T0114664

Rescued
Redeemed
Raptured

KATHERINE MICHELLE WOODS

authorHOUSE®

AuthorHouse™
1663 Liberty Drive
Bloomington, IN 47403
www.authorhouse.com
Phone: 833-262-8899

Published by AuthorHouse 04/27/2023

ISBN: 979-8-8230-0628-6 (sc)
ISBN: 979-8-8230-0627-9 (e)

Print information available on the last page.

This book is printed on acid-free paper.

Contents

After writing my book "All Children Are Mine," several people wanted me to continue the saga about our brave young Christian children. Their encounters are all similar, yet they all have different experiences. Their faith is tested; although facing persecution and even death, they remain steadfast in their devotion to Jesus. They exhibit unfaltering Christian values through their actions, thus attracting other people to faith in Jesus. Revelation 3:10 tells us that because you have kept your command to persevere, I will also keep you from the hour trial which shall come upon the entire world, to test those who dwell on the earth. Our crusaders experience the "Rapture of the Church" based on 1 Thessalonians 4:16-18. People they encounter either accept Jesus Christ and are redeemed, or they reject Jesus.

There are two principles I wish to convey. The first principle, God is faithful to forgive anyone of any offense, no matter the grievousness of that offense. The person must sincerely repent and ask Jesus to be the Lord of their life. There are consequences for our rejection and rebellion against Jesus, which is the second principle. These consequences affect everyone in our sphere of influence.

I especially want to thank my daughter Dr. Susan Gaffney for her assistance and my brother Michael Griffin. May God bless you and keep you. I pray you will enjoy my book.

Rescue – Protected

Psalm 17: 8 and 9

8 Keep me as the apple of Your eye;

Hide me under the shadow of Your wings,

9 From the wicked who oppress me,

From my deadly enemies who surround me.

Psalm 91

1 He who dwells in the secret place of the Most High

Shall abide under the shadow of the Almighty.

2 I will say of the Lord, "He is my refuge and my fortress;

My God, in Him I will trust."

3 Surely He shall deliver you from the snare of the fowler

And from the perilous pestilence.

4 He shall cover you with His feathers,

And under His wings you shall take refuge;

His truth shall be your shield and [b]buckler.

5 You shall not be afraid of the terror by night,

Nor of the arrow that flies by day,

6 Nor of the pestilence that walks in darkness,

Nor of the destruction that lays waste at noonday.

7 A thousand may fall at your side,

And ten thousand at your right hand;

But it shall not come near you.

8 Only with your eyes shall you look,

And see the reward of the wicked.

9 Because you have made the Lord, who is my refuge,

Even the Most High, your dwelling place,

10 No evil shall befall you,

Nor shall any plague come near your dwelling;

11 For He shall give His angels charge over you,

To keep you in all your ways.

12 In their hands they shall bear you up,

Lest you dash your foot against a stone.

13 You shall tread upon the lion and the cobra,

The young lion and the serpent you shall trample underfoot.

14 "Because he has set his love upon Me, therefore I will deliver him;

I will set him on high, because he has known My name.

15 He shall call upon Me, and I will answer him;

I will be with him in trouble;

I will deliver him and honor him.

16 With long life, I will satisfy him,

And show him My salvation."

2 Thessalonians 3:3

But the Lord is faithful, who will establish you and guard you from the evil one.

Isaiah 41:10

10 Fear not, for I am with you;

Be not dismayed, for I am your God.
I will strengthen you,
Yes, I will help you,
I will uphold you with My righteous right hand.'

Isaiah 54:17

17 No weapon formed against you shall prosper,
And every tongue which rises against you in judgment
You shall condemn.
This is the heritage of the servants of the Lord,
And their righteousness is from Me,"
Says the Lord.

Redemption

Acts 3:19

19 Repent therefore and be converted, that your sins may be blotted out, so that times of refreshing may come from the presence of the Lord.

Ephesians 1:7

7 Fear not, for I am with you;
Be not dismayed, for I am your God.
I will strengthen you,
Yes, I will help you,
I will uphold you with My righteous right hand.

Galatians 1:4

4 Who gave Himself for our sins, that He might deliver us from this present evil age, according to the will of our God and Father,

Galatians 2:20

20 I have been crucified with Christ; it is no longer I who live, but Christ lives in me; and the life which I now live in the flesh I live by faith in the Son of God, who loved me and gave Himself for me.

Hebrews 9:15

15 And for this reason He is the Mediator of the new covenant, by means of death, for the redemption of the transgressions under the first covenant, that those who are called may receive the promise of the eternal inheritance.

Isaiah 44:22

22 I have blotted out, like a thick cloud, your transgressions,
And like a cloud, your sins.
Return to Me, for I have redeemed you."

John 3:16

16 For God so loved the world that He gave His only begotten Son, that whoever believes in Him should not perish but have everlasting life.

Rapture

I Corinthians 15: 51-52

51 Behold, I tell you a [m]mystery: We shall not all sleep, but we shall all be changed— 52 in a moment, in the twinkling of an eye, at the last trumpet. For the trumpet will sound, and the dead will be raised incorruptible, and we shall be changed.

Matthew 24:40-41 40

40 Then two men will be in the field: one will be taken and the other left. 41 Two women will be grinding at the mill: one will be taken and the other left.

I Thessalonians 4:16 – 18

16 For the Lord Himself will descend from heaven with a shout, with the voice of an archangel, and with the trumpet of God. And the dead in Christ will rise first. 17 Then we who are alive and remain shall be caught up together with them in the clouds to meet the Lord in the air. And thus, we shall always be with the Lord. 18 Therefore comfort one another with these words.

Chapter 1

EUMAI: PROTECTED

I was eight years old the first time you met me. Eumai is my name. Living in a society under communist rule with a supreme leader, a dictator, has not been easy; however, God has protected my family and me all these years. I have become stronger in my faith and my daily walk with Jesus.

When there was an attempted robbery of a soldier, an extremely rare event in my country where people are afraid to look at a soldier directly in the face, a manhunt was initiated immediately. The soldier described a teenage girl dressed in black pants and a puffy blue coat; he said she attempted to grab his weapon. I just happened to be returning from the university where I was taught advanced technical skills. Surveillance cameras did not capture the offender's face; however, she was wearing the exact color coat and pants that I was wearing. I wear this combination of clothing almost every day; I only have four wardrobe choices.

Five heavily armed soldiers came to my home, arrested me, and took me to a work camp. There was no trial or even an interrogation. Trembling and crying, I prayed to Jesus, and I kept asking Him why this was happening to me, a devout Christian who stood up for Jesus despite the perils I faced in this atheist, communist dictatorship. While praying on my knees in my tiny cell, an angel appeared. I knew him!

He had saved my father from death and our whole family from possible imprisonment. The angel spoke to me this time. "Beloved daughter, you have been chosen by the Most High to witness to your fellow prisoners and the guards; they are without hope because they do not know Jesus. You must teach them God's word and help them know that Jesus will forgive and save them. Many souls will be saved because of your obedience and exemplary dedication to Jesus. Do not fear, for this demonic regime will be toppled before very long. God will protect you. He will place a wall of protection around you, and you will be shown favor." I felt how Joseph must have felt when he was wrongfully imprisoned in Egypt, but he was shown favor in prison and later became the second in command of all Egypt.

Ten years have passed, and I am still imprisoned in the work camp; however, I eat and drink the same food as the soldiers. It is not the most nutritious food but healthier than inmates' food. I do not do hard labor because I excel in computer skills I learned while attending university. The soldiers have never attacked me, beat me, or sexually violated me. I continue to witness to the soldiers and my fellow detainees. No one has ever betrayed me to the authorities. God has built a shield of protection all around me. I do not know when or if I will be set free, but I know that Jesus will continue to sustain me through this lengthy trial. Praise God! Praise God!

DUCK-HWAN: REDEEMED

I am Duck-Hwan; my name means return of virtue. You would not believe how accurately this meaning describes my life. Remember when a soldier took the groceries from a man who had just purchased food to feed his poor family. I am ashamed to say that soldier was me: a mean, disgruntled, selfish, starving soldier. Making excuses for myself is not my intention because I know I was dead wrong. Despicable would be the adjective to describe me until I saw that colossal angel that appeared between that young father and me. Since that day, I started seeking to know who sent the angel to protect that family. To my surprise, I discovered there is an underground Christian church here in our atheist country. Christians or Christ followers pray to Jesus for not only protection but for joy and eternal life. I know their Jesus answers prayer.

Several of my fellow soldiers attend this underground church. The guards at the work camp told me about this lady in custody, who is probably innocent. She is fearless, and God has shown her favor: she does not suffer from sickness or depression. Her faith is steadfast. She eats the same food the soldiers eat, not that we get ample food, but it is better quality than what the prisoners eat. The food is awful because it is grown using untreated human excrement for fertilizer. We are not allowed to buy regular fertilizer because of sanctions against us imposed by western nations because of our relentless quest for nuclear weapons. Soldiers' food rations are minimal, and there is no nutritional value. Hunger pangs and muscle fatigue are commonplace among soldiers because of war drills and endless practice for parades. Eleven years of mandatory military service for men and seven years for women are required.

When I finally met Eumai, the Christian lady who works in the prison office, it was difficult to convince her that I was not a spy. She recognized me as the soldier who took her father's groceries; however, she finally accepted me into her underground Bible study. The Bible class was fantastic, eye-opening, and enlightening.

After several weeks of learning about Father God, the Lord Jesus, and the Holy Spirit, I sincerely repented and asked Jesus to be the Lord and Savior of my life. Although my circumstances have not changed, my heart has changed. I love people and look for opportunities to help and encourage them. Praying to Jesus every day has become my routine. I know Jesus will deliver us from this godless, oppressive regime through natural or supernatural means. Our souls have been spiritually redeemed, and I believe our physical bodies will also be redeemed.

EUMAI: RAPTURE

I am Eumai, and this is the last time you will hear from me; never being released from work camp imprisonment, I decided to allow Jesus to lead me without complaining. Almost half of the soldiers who guard the camps are saved now, and many prisoners are also saved. Although the guards cannot openly admit they are saved, they do not mistreat prisoners and genuinely attempt to help them. All citizens are sick; they suffer from diarrhea, dysentery, hookworm, and a host of other diseases. However, God has granted me good health, although I have been hungry lately.

The Apostle Paul tells us in Philippians 4:12 that we should be content in whatever state we find ourselves in, "I know what it is to be in need, and I know what it is to have plenty. I have learned the secret of being content in any and every situation, whether well fed or hungry, whether living in plenty or in want." I decided not to worry about being hungry anymore. Recently I found that even our supreme leader was sick. Some soldiers are feeble; they cannot even carry their weapons. Why this is happening is a mystery to me. Maybe this is what the angel was referencing when he said this regime would be toppled. I never thought it would happen this way.

Several prisoners were released, and I was allowed to teach Bible class openly. One day a Christian officer told me to go home and get my family, and he would lead us across the demilitarized zone to freedom. My parents and other relatives were overjoyed to see me. After warmly greeting each other, we leisurely walked to our new country and our new life. All you could hear was loud praise and rejoicing. Relatives greeted us, and wonderful Christian people fed, clothed, and provided comfortable living quarters in our new country.

After a few weeks in what seemed like a utopia, we attended church service in real brick-and-mortar churches. There were so many Christians who loved us. The entire congregation thanked Jesus for our freedom.

Hours passed, and we were still rejoicing, praying, and crying tears of joy when we heard someone shouting; it sounded like it was coming from the North. Suddenly, we heard what sounded like several horns. Were the soldiers from the North going to start shooting us? Our names were being called. Then "It" happened; we were "caught up" in the air! The "Rapture of the Church" was occurring. We were snatched so quickly; I cannot explain it. My head was whirling. There is nothing to which I can compare it. Our clothes were different. When did that happen? We were wearing loose-fitting, comfortable robes. As we flew higher and higher, I thought about my life. I did not have one regret. Although I was never married, had children, or even graduated from the university, I am fulfilled and thankful that God counted me worthy to bring so many souls to Him. After what seemed like a long time, I saw bright lights. There were people and angels in the sky. A sparkling city was before us, and then I saw the most beautiful sight of all. Jesus was standing on a cloud with His arms open, welcoming us home.

Chapter 2

MARGARET: PROTECTED

Iam Margaret, and I feel privileged to be alive and well. If you will remember, Jesus Himself touched me and instantly healed me when I had only days to live. My parents and I got saved. After quitting their lucrative jobs, we all relocated to a remote village in Africa, where my parents began their ministry. Then we met a marvelous, outstanding, formidable doctor/evangelist; she was originally from Jamaica. Her name was Dr. Coril Endego. God directed her to stay in Africa longer after ministering in another village for two years. Dr. Coril had to help navigate another village through an Ebola epidemic. We were shocked to find out this epidemic had just started the week before we arrived.

We all survived because we followed Dr. Coril's instructions exactly, giving attention to every detail. The other doctors, nurses, and volunteers who followed their own plan perished. After the Ebola crisis finally ended, we devoted all of our efforts to fighting the influence of Voodoo.

Most of the villagers believed in the Voodoo religion. A supreme being named Zeriba, who is supposedly all-powerful, yet detached from human affairs, controls everyone through mighty witch doctors. These witch doctors dictate the behavior of the villagers through fear and intimidation. After Dr. Coril and my parents continued preaching the gospel to villagers, most of them accepted Jesus as their Lord and Savior. The witch doctors harassed us constantly with spells, incantations, and other forms of witchcraft. Needless to say, "no weapons formed against us prospered."

One night a newly converted lady told my parents that the witchdoctors from several villages were joining forces to come after our children. They planned on summoning all of their demonic powers to recruit the children in our village to become their apprentices. When we found out the date of the devil's wicket initiative, we began fasting and praying. We believed James 5:16: "The effectual fervent praying of a righteous man availed much." We were determined to pray until we all felt assured that God heard us and that God Almighty would put a stop to their plans.

A few days later, at midnight, the shamans gathered in the middle of the main road where most villagers lived. Multi-generational families occupied their modest homes with several young children. The witch doctors were all decked out in their scary masks, feathered costumes, and layers of make-up. They started beating their drums and making animal noises. They prayed to some demonic deity named Zeriba. Children came out of their homes as they began chanting and repeating their demonic mantra. As the witch doctors beat their drums louder and chanted louder, more children were summoned to follow them. The noise was almost deafening, and the children looked as if they were in a trance; they looked like zombies. Parents attempted to restrain them; the children pushed their parents aside. It was surreal. I could not believe what was happening. All the Christians gathered at one end of the street and started praying aloud. "Jesus, deliver us for your name's sake. We are yours. No demons in hell are more powerful than you. Save your children." Demonic forces confronting Christian forces on a village street at midnight was bizarre.

Suddenly it started to rain. The raindrops became hailstones the size of golf balls. The hail did not come near us. Picture a long street where the forces of darkness are being pummeled with golf ball size hailstones, and at the other end of the street, the Christians are not even wet from the rain; the sky above was completely clear. Remember the plagues of Egypt where the Egyptians were suffering plague after plague, and the Hebrews did not experience any of them. I thought about Psalm 91, where it said, "a thousand may fall at your side and ten thousand at your right hand, no evil will come near your dwelling." We watched as hailstones battered the witch doctors until some of them were bloody and severely wounded. Some hailstones struck them so forcibly that they died from severe head trauma. Several of them looked up and shook their fist at God; hail stones battered their eyes and blinded them. How foolish could they get! After what seemed like a long time, the children came back to their senses and walked into their houses. We all cried tears of joy and thanked God, confident that the witch doctors would not attempt to revisit children from our village again.

I am studying to become a doctor and a missionary, just like Dr. Coril. I have decided to devote my life to serving God in countries whose economies are emerging. Money and power mean absolutely nothing unless you use your money to serve God by helping His children. Glory be to God.

MARGARET: RAPTURE

Hello again, I am Margaret, who Jesus himself healed from an incurable disease. You last heard from me when I was in Africa with my parents, fighting Ebola and mighty witch doctors. We were successful because of God's grace and Dr. Coril and her staff. After graduating from medical school in London, I decided to emulate Dr. Coril by practicing medicine and being an evangelist in an emerging economy country. I married Dr. Coril's grandson Declan; he is so handsome and such a talented surgeon. I feel so blessed to be married to him because we share the same vision of ministering to poor villagers medically and spiritually. We are both saved and filled with God's Holy Spirit. Where we live in New Guinea, there is a small hospital and a small grocery store. Most of the people live in small villages and hamlets. The natives use the available materials to build their homes, for example, wood, and grasses. Most of them have thatched roofs. Our days are long and arduous.

Believe it or not, some villagers were still practicing cannibalism, and some believed in animism and ancestor worship. A few villagers suffered from Kura disease because of digesting human flesh. Kura disease is also called laughing disease because sufferers laugh spontaneously. Villagers who practiced animism believed that everything has a soul:

plants, animals, and objects. Ancestor worshippers believe their ancestors maintain a spiritual connection with them forever. Our villagers also suffered from some common diseases in their area: malaria, respiratory diseases, diarrhea, and diseases related to HIV/AIDS from heterosexual contact.

After several years of intense Bible study and continuous prayer and fasting, our villagers no longer practiced cannibalism. They no longer believe you have to eat the flesh of another human being who was demon-possessed, or because you loved and respected them. Our townspeople no longer believe in animism; however, some still practice ancestor worship.

Subsistent farming and fishing are the two main occupations. The farmers grow sage, sweet potatoes, leafy greens, coconut, and fruit. On special occasions, they eat pork. Declan and I went fishing with several members of our extended family. I hooked a huge fish, but I was catapulted overboard when I attempted to reel it in. A shark came toward me and bit off my leg. My husband jumped in to save me. The blood must have drawn more sharks to the area. Another shark bit my husband's foot. We had no idea the waterway was shark infested. Our native friends jumped into the water and used oars to beat the sharks in the gills and eyes. They rescued us and transported us to our small hospital. We maintained our emergency staff of one doctor, three physician assistants, and ten nurses. They all worked feverishly to save our lives.

We were not nearly as productive as we were before, we had to navigate with amputated limbs; however, we were thankful to be alive and to care for our patients. People from around the world sent us emails telling us what an inspiration we were because we chose to stay in our village and not to be offended by God for allowing the sharks to attack us. I must admit sometimes we were depressed and disillusioned; we contemplated moving to a more populated modern location or even back to Europe or the United States.

Late one night, we were awakened from a deep sleep by shouting. "Wake up, Listen." Whoever it was certainly had our attention. We heard our names being called. Was it the cannibals from the neighboring villages? Were they coming after us because we helped to convert our people to Christianity? Were they going to boil and devour us? We heard our names clearly. "Declan and Margaret, come up here." There was a loud blast from a horn: a trumpet. The music blared louder and louder. Before I could even look around, I realized I was being whisked through the roof of our house. I noticed my leg had been regenerated; the prosthetic leg was gone. My husband's foot was also regenerated. I started laughing; I could not express how much joy I was experiencing. We were flying at warp speed with hands stretched out in front. Several of our villagers were also being Raptured. What were we wearing? We had on robes with sashes around our waist. The sky was filled with people in long beautiful white robes. Everyone looked young and healthy. We looked like birds with white plumage. We kept flying upward; we seemed to be escorted by angels. Finally, we reached our destination. Jesus Christ was standing on a cloud, smiling the most beautiful smile I have ever seen.

AVARE ABEBE: REDEMPTION

You do not really know me, but I will tell you what happened to me. I am Avare Abebe, and I was a powerful witch doctor. My family had promised the god Zeriba that I would be his dedicated servant when I was born. After what happened to me when those Christians started praying against us to their God, I was not confident about Zerbia's power. Their God, the Creator of the universe, beat me until I was bloody using giant hailstones. My evil cabal and I attempted to recruit children to serve Zeriba. After God's display of majesty and dominance, I was confused and disillusioned; then, I got angry. I intended on showing those Christians who was in charge. I would murder a famous evangelist who was coming to a nearby village to conduct a crusade for Jesus. Since the crusade would be televised, I planned to cut his throat in view of an international audience. I would pretend to be healed; I would be escorted to the platform to give my testimony about my miraculous healing. When evangelist Kenthart gave me the microphone, I would cut his throat. No one would have faith in Jesus anymore. They would choose to return to Zeriba for protection. If there were metal detectors, I would bring a ceramic knife with a blade as sharp as a razor hidden in my shirt sleeve.

The worship music began, and all of the Christians were singing, raising their hands in worship, crying, and praising Jesus. They were falling under the power of the Holy Spirit. I knew their God was powerful, but I intended on diminishing His power by killing His evangelist. His worshipers were phony actors paid by the evangelist anyway. Zeriba was about to show them who was master and chief in this world. Well, events did not quite happen the way I had intended. When one of the pastors got close to me, I pretended to faint under the power of the Holy Spirit. I did not give him a chance to touch me or pray for me. When I was called to the platform, I walked up there confidently with murder in my heart. As soon as I stepped on that stage, I was accosted by three big, burly pastors. They barely touched me, and I collapsed like a house of cards. I was lying on the ground, burning up inside. I heard someone say, "demons of hell come out of him in the name of Jesus Christ." They repeated it several times. I felt like the air was being released from my lungs; I felt lighter, as if I had lost twenty pounds. When I became fully conscious, I looked around as someone pulled me to my feet. Thousands of people stretched their arms toward me and prayed in some unknown languages.

I started crying and laughing. I jumped up and down. I leaped over that stage. I was free. I heard myself saying thank you to Jesus repeatedly. How could I have been so deceived and bound up by Satan all those years? I kept asking Jesus to forgive me and save me. Everyone started cheering for me. Soon I was speaking in an unknown language. I was saved and filled with the Holy Spirit!

Everyone should experience this love and freedom freely given to us by Jesus. I aligned myself with this wonderful ministry, traveling with them to conduct crusades everywhere. Pastors Adoje told me that an angel had warned him about me in a dream. He said the angel described me and told him that I had a knife in my sleeve to kill Evangelist Kenthart. He warned two other evangelists and told them to tackle me when I stood on the platform. I am so thankful that God saved me. It was unbelievable how a righteous God could save me. I tortured people physically and emotionally. I conjured spells to cause people to become blind, crippled, and deaf. I kidnapped children and dared their parents to stop me. If Jesus can forgive me, He can forgive you. I now attempt to persuade other witchdoctors and Voodoo worshippers to come to Jesus. They constantly threaten me; but I will continue giving my testimony to everyone who will listen. I tell them about the power of Jesus. I tell them that I am redeemed.

Chapter 3

MARCUS: REDEEMED

Hello everyone, I am Marcus. If you recall, a shooter attempted to kill Deandra while he and his sister Laquisha were sitting on their porch. I am that shooter. If that angel had not intervened, my story would have turned out quite differently. After I ran off that porch and returned to our car, affectionately known as a "ganstaship." I was shaken; I could not stop trembling and making sobbing sounds. Who would have believed an enormous angel would appear out of nowhere and catch a bullet in midair that was flying toward Deandre's head?

I had noticed Deandre's family going to that Apostolic church at the corner, near their house. I also lived very close to that church. You must understand my mindset to comprehend my values fully. My mother was a materialistic person who equated expensive clothes and jewelry with having achieved the American dream. Consequently, I judged people by their outward appearance. Deandre's family dressed in cheap clothes. Their mother wore cheap dresses and hats to church, their dad wore poor fitting suits, and their children never wore designer athletic shoes or clothing. Why would someone envy them? I envied them because they were a family who went to church several times a week; they seemed happy although they lived in an old house and their dad drove an old car. They had no luxuries, but they had each other and faith in Jesus.

I never knew my dad because he was in prison for being a drug dealer and a murderer. I had no siblings and no relatives. It was just my mother and me against the world. There are plenty of single mothers who can adequately raise a teenage African American male, but my mother just was not one of them. Her dad died when she was eleven years old, and her mother became a heroin addict who allowed my mom to be sexually abused continually by my grandmother's numerous boyfriends. My mom left home at sixteen years old and never looked back. She never forgave her mother or other relatives for not rescuing her from a living hell. Emotionally damaged with little self-esteem, she hooked -up with my dad, who lavished her with furs, diamonds, and money. When she became pregnant with me, she begged my dad to marry her; he never got around to it.

My dad was serving a life sentence before I was born. I knew my mom loved me because she worked at a meatpacking company to provide a decent living for us. She left home at five-thirty in the morning to work her seven-thirty to three-thirty shift so she could be home by the time school was over for me. She helped me with my homework and even paid a tutor to help me in math. My mom cooked during the week; but treated us to Red Lobster, Olive Garden, and the Cheesecake Factory on the weekends. My birthdays were spectacular: presents, presents, presents! On Christmas, I also received expensive gifts.

I had two best friends who were always invited to my small yet wonderful birthday parties. My friend's parents, my mom, and I spent most holidays together. I missed not having a dad; however, life was great.

Life was not wonderful for long. My friends moved to other states because the city was just too dangerous, too much gang violence. Little did they know, and little did I know that they were moving away because of me. I was about to become a gangster, a banger. My high school experience was dismal. Everything that could go wrong did go wrong.

My mother and I made a series of bad decisions. Escalating gang violence, especially in the early morning hours, caused my mom to change her work schedule; she began working from 3:30 pm until 11:30 pm. She was able to get a ride home at night. She could not afford a Cadillac Escalade, a Mercedes, or a Jaguar. Purchasing a Chevrolet, Nissan, or Toyota was not fly enough for her. How warped is that reasoning? She would rather take public transportation! The truth is mom would prefer spending all of her money buying designer clothes for herself and me: no bank account and no emergency funds.

My mother never had a boyfriend or even a male friend because she was afraid someone would abuse me the way she was abused. I asked her why we did not attend church. Mom explained that she had attempted to join several churches through the years, but they always asked too many questions. When were you baptized, and what other churches have you joined? Do you have relatives or friends who are members? It was just too humiliating. If they only knew that no one in my mom's family ever owned a Bible. Mom gave up too quickly.

I needed a male role model: a cousin, an uncle, a family male friend, my dad. I was not allowed to talk to my dad on the telephone and certainly not visit while he was in prison. If I had talked to my dad, maybe he would have warned me about the pitfalls that lay ahead of me.

There was no plan for me from three-thirty in the afternoon until my mom got home at midnight. My mom never asked me what subject I liked in school; or even if I liked a certain girl. How could she have been so protective when I was in elementary school and when I needed guidance, my mom provided no oversight? There was a real missed opportunity for my mom to watch over me. When her boss brought his fourteen-year-old son to work with him from three-thirty p.m. until eleven-thirty p.m., explaining to his employees that he had to make sure his son was supervised at all times as a single parent. If he were not legally able to pay him, he would give him a stipend. Why didn't Mom speak up and ask if she could bring me to work with her? Was she ashamed of me? Was she afraid I would talk about my father? Was she afraid I would be opposed to going to work with her? I do not know! So, what if I did not want to go; I was the child. She was the parent. My mother never attempted to enroll me in an after-school program at the Boys and Girls Club. She and I never discussed my poor grades or my long-term plans for the future. She always complimented me about how I matched my beautiful designer clothes. I knew she loved me because she constantly told me how much she loved me and that I was all she had: however, my mom did not equip me to survive. Would you send a soldier to war without weapons? Would you leave a defenseless infant in the jungle? I needed her to teach me, watch me, and counsel me. I was ripe for the picking: a sheep in a den of wolves. Well, those are a few of my mom's bad decisions; now, I will tell you about my bad decisions and my failure to listen to that inward voice attempting to warn me of impending danger.

If I were completely honest, I did not even attempt to find out what subject interested me. Being too short to play basketball, too small to play football or wrestle, and too slow to run track, I did not attempt to engage in any sport. I could have played tennis, fencing, or even chess. Lazy and spoiled would accurately describe my character. I was bored and restless. I could have worked as a bagger at the grocery store, a stock boy at Walmart, or the Home Deport, even a concession worker at the movie theater. I thought I was too good to earn minimum wage. The days of Marcus' troubles were about to begin.

I was standing outside on the steps of the school when I should have been in English class; I noticed a big old car parked in front of the school. Three people were inside; two of them went out periodically to talk to students passing by. One day a boy about my age exited the car and asked me if I wanted to get high on weed, free of charge. I felt a foreboding; a small, still voice warning me to stay away; that had never happened to me before. At first, I refused, remembering my grandmother's addiction and my father's plight because of drugs. After several weeks, I got in the car and smoked weed for the first time. Surprisingly it did not impress me; I just got a little buzzed. An older guy was sitting in the backseat. He had a huge gold dog tag around his neck, his name in gold letters surrounded by diamonds. He wore a beautiful Rolex watch. Big Hommey was his name, and he was the leader of a notorious street gang. He flattered me, telling me how exquisitely I dressed. He asked me how many pairs of Timberlands and Jordans I owned; I told him I had two of each. They all laughed as he gave me eight boxes of shoes, four pairs of Jordans, and four pairs of Timberlands in different colors. They were my size. He pulled off his Rolex and put it on my skinny arm, telling me we would have to take out a few links. I thanked him, but I refused the gifts. That same inside voice told me to get out of the car immediately. I did not obey because I was intrigued and beguiled. I took the gifts.

Several weeks passed before I saw the big car in front of the school; maybe I just avoided going outside during English class. Big Hommey summoned me to the car. I was afraid not to go. Once inside the car, Big

Hommey's demeanor changed as he told me that it was time for me to pay my debt. He said I owed him about four thousand dollars. Looking confused, I explained that I did not have any money and thought the gifts were a present. He explained that I would pay my debt and ensure my loyalty to his organization by following his instructions implicitly. First, my gang and I would burglarize high-end stores at night, stealing expensive merchandise while the stores were unoccupied. Our burglaries would escalate to daytime crimes. Soon we would be required to rob people at gunpoint. Next, we would be expected to carjack, especially if a luxury automobile was accessible.

Finally, we would have to choose a menu item: an entrée. I was utterly confused, but I knew I could not do any of the horrible, despicable acts he had described. My head started reeling. Explaining that I could not do these things was futile. Big Hommey held up a hammer and told me that he would knock out every tooth in my mouth if I even hesitated not to obey him. If I still were not convinced, he would kill my mother, and then he would kill me. Big Hommey carefully explained to me that choosing an appetizer meant that I had to maim someone; choosing an entrée meant that I had to murder someone up-front and personal. One of my crew members would photograph events to ensure my loyalty and prevent me from going to the police. If I failed to comply, I would be considered a traitor. Traitors and rival gang members were killed in an especially heinous manner; they were considered a dessert. There was one bright light at the end of the tunnel; I would be tried as a juvenile if I were to be apprehended by law enforcement because I was only fourteen. My sentence would be a few years.

I could not breathe; I started hyperventilating. Big Hommey lovingly told me to cup my hands and breathe slowly into my palms. He called me Baby Boy and told me that I would be just fine. I knew the name Baby Boy was a derogatory remark. I saw the movie about a teenage boy who was irresponsible, lazy, reckless, and dependent on his mother. That description seemed to fit me. I was so afraid; to whom could I talk about all this? There was no one: not a policeman, a teacher, a pastor, or my dad. I knew my mom could not help me.

We could never relocate because mom earned a good salary for a high-school drop-out; mom was not a skilled worker. She had worked at the company for thirteen long years: never being late or absent, no matter the weather conditions. Monetary raises, days off, and a supervisory position rewarded her perseverance and dedication. What kind of viable solution could she offer? I neither slept nor ate for three days. I cried, I laughed.

I talked to myself. I found myself talking to Jesus, although I did not know him, and I did not deserve His help. I knew about Jesus. My friend's parents attended church and put their lives in Jesus' hands. I had nothing to lose by praying to Jesus. It seemed as if Jesus had ignored me, but, later I realized Jesus was orchestrating events so Big Hommey would kick me out of the gang without making me a dessert item.

Big Hommey had already mapped out our criminal agenda. First, we burglarized two high-end stores on the Gold Coast. Leroy was proficient at breaking into stores and disarming security systems. Our first haul yielded Louis Vuitton, Herme, and Valentino ladies' handbags. Needles to say, the lion's share went to Big Hommey, and we divided the remaining purses. We burglarized a jewelry store where Leroy adeptly broke into a safe. Leroy was a criminal genius.

I gave my mom handbags and jewelry. She only asked one time where I was getting all the expensive items. Ridiculous! I told her some boy at school found them and was selling them cheaply. She knew I was lying; some African American single mothers cannot raise an African American male child. I even forgot to hide my gun one night; my mother saw it. She did not question me about it.

After a few weeks of burglarizing high-end stores, we were ordered to start carjacking. Carjacking required a whole new set of skills. However, there were crimes of opportunity, most successful carjacking involved time and patience. I learned what the word reconnaissance means: observing a region to locate an enemy or ascertain strategic features. The carjacking victim was the enemy. We always looked for an opportunity first. If a person appeared old with gray hair or if they had a slow gait or handicap, they were a target. My crew and I would choose a middle-class neighborhood. In wealthy areas, car owners tended to buy automobiles that were more challenging to steal. The BMW, Range Rover, Tesla, and Jaguar had complicated anti-theft software. We focused on the Jeep Cherokee, Dodge and GMC pick-ups, Toyota Corolla and Camry, and Nissans. They were easier to steal and dismantle through trial and error. The parts could be sold for more than the vehicle's initial cost. Big Hommey wanted us to be fearless and ruthless, so we had to carjack instead of just stealing an unoccupied vehicle.

We would park at the end of the block and observe the driving habits of the neighborhood residents. When people parked in their driveway, it was easy for us to pull up behind them and demand their keys, threatening them with a revolver. When people backed into the garage, it was a nightmare for us. They could see us approaching and run us down. Leroy suffered two broken legs when the intended victim drove out of the garage and hit him. Attempting to carjack someone once they had driven into the garage was also dangerous. Once the driver took a gun from his car glove compartment and started shooting at us. We barely escaped. Often, we would follow someone after they left the house. If they stopped for a traffic light and no one was around, we would carjack them. Usually, they took the same route each day. Carjacking became a fun sport; we were living on the edge. We had become depraved, feeling no sympathy for older people or younger people trying to make an honest living driving to work or the grocery store.

The carjacking was terrible enough; then, we were told to rob people downtown in the daytime. Are you beginning to sense a feeling of mistrust for Big Hommey? Did he want us to get caught or killed? I attempted to rob someone by brandishing my gun. The man looked at my one-hundred forty-five-pound body and laughed as he knocked the gun from my hand. He ran when he saw my boys running toward me. Leroy and Delance said they would not tell Big Hommey because he would hurt my mother. It was decided that I would be the designated driver. I was relieved not to rob someone and threaten to shoot them. I never thought I could do something like that, but I did it that one time.

The next crime we had to commit was horrendous. We had to do drive-by shootings. It was such a despicable act that Leroy and Delance had to snort cocaine before they prowled for someone or a group of innocent people to murder. I had to drive. My posse pretended they were playing a violent video game. They shot so many innocent people, men, women, and children. I was about ready to commit suicide because I did not see a way out. The next day Big Hommey decided our drive-by days had ended. It was time to choose our entrée.

I chose Deandre as my entrée because I envied him so much. He had a loving family, excelled academically, and was a good athlete. He even tutored other students in math two days a week. All the pretty girls loved him; they flocked around, giggling and grabbing his arm. I wanted to be him, not murder him. For the first time in my life, I got down on my knees and prayed to Jesus for four hours. I confessed all my sins. I admitted admiring how adept Leroy was at breaking in stores and disarming alarm systems. He could open a safe in a few minutes. I enjoyed watching Delance and Leroy rob people and carjack people before the victims realized what was happening to them. Giving my mom expensive gifts made me feel wonderful. I lived in a fantasy world, but now events were about to become very real. I poured out my heart to Jesus

33

and implored Him to intervene on my behalf or to give me the courage to commit suicide. While I was still on my knees, a feeling of peace came over me. Although I had never experienced this feeling before, I knew that everything would be okay. I did not know how Jesus was going to save Deandre and me, but I knew that he would.

As I stepped out of the car that day, I wondered why Jesus had not caused us to have an engine failure or why Jesus had not caused us to be involved in a serious accident. As I climbed the steps to Deandre's porch, I wondered why I did not fall through a broken step. Why didn't Delance call Leroy and I back to the car because Big Hommey had been killed in a gang shooting? As I aimed the gun at Deandre's head, why didn't it fall from my hand? Why didn't my hand become paralyzed?

I never expected Jesus to send an angel to catch the bullet aimed at Deandre's head! After I saw that enormous angel catch my bullet, I ran to our ganstaship with Leroy hot on my heels. Delance did not know what happened, but he quickly drove us to Big Hommey's house. Trembling and uttering incoherent words was all Big Hommey saw and heard. Leroy showed him the picture with my finger on the trigger and a big white light next to Deandre when he asked what had happened. Leroy was mute, and his skin was ashen. Finally, Leroy was able to describe what happened in broken phrases. For the first time in one year, I saw fear on Big Hommey's face. He told me that I would never be of any use to him and that I could leave the gang without any repercussions. Leroy could leave also; he decided to stay.

My poor attendance caused me to be booted out of high school. I took the initiative to enroll myself in an alternative high school. I excelled in carpentry, and I learned to build good sturdy furniture. After three years, I graduated and became an apprentice at a furniture outlet factory. To my surprise, I held my own with the rest of the employees by following my mother's example of being an exemplary employee. I was promoted to a supervisory position. The most important decision I made was to join the Apostolic church at the corner near my house. I only glimpsed Deandre and Laquita now and then. I made sure they did not see me. I got saved, and my mother attended church with me. My mom always said she would only consider joining that church because no one asked her personal questions about her past. Some people dressed nicely, and some did not; nevertheless, they all worshiped together joyfully. They seemed like a real church family.

One day while walking to my house. I noticed an old car, our ganstaship. The auto was parked across the street where a group of young girls jumped rope, and a young teenage boy passed by the girls. He had a backpack and earphones on his ears, oblivious to his surroundings. I assessed the situation instantly. Leroy exited the car with a gun in his hand; it was a semi-automatic submachine gun. I could hardly believe it. He intended to spray the whole area. What was the point? Did he want to do something to propel himself to become the next Big Hommey? Before I had time to think about it, I called out to Leroy while I ran toward him. I must have frightened him because he looked at me as if he did not recognize me, and he pulled the trigger aiming at my heart: at that moment, the trajectory of the bullet changed. It turned about ninety degrees and struck me in my right shoulder instead of my heart. The pain was excruciating. My shoulder felt as if it were on fire. The next thing I remembered was waking up in the hospital to the smiling face of my mother and Pastor Bryon. The Lord Jesus had caused the bullet to change directions; thus, saving my life. After my close call, my mom got saved, realizing that Jesus loves us and that he can protect us.

My shoulder was shattered, but thankfully I did not have to build furniture anymore. I just supervised others without hands-on demonstrations. As I look back over my life. I realize that all actions have consequences for you and other people in your life. It did me no good to wish my mom had married a saved man and not gotten involved with my father. I wished I had read the Bible and learned about teenagers like Joseph, Daniel, Shadrach, Meshach, and Abednego, who faced temptations and were victorious because of their faith in God. I am so thankful that God is a God of second chances. It is difficult to fathom that God forgives all your sins if you sincerely repent and ask Jesus to be the Lord of your life. If I could live a thousand lifetimes, I could never repay God for sparing me and sending Jesus to die for my sins. I can do something to prevent young impressionable teens from being duped into a life of crime. I mentor young boys at my church; I teach them to recognize gang leaders as predators. I have learned that all people who are saved and love Jesus are rich beyond measure. Material possessions mean absolutely nothing. That day when Jesus sent the angel to save Deandre's life, he also saved my life. I am redeemed.

DEANDRE: RAPTURED

I am Deandre, whom you met several years ago when an angel caught a bullet aimed at my head fired at close range. My sister and I learned to call on the Lord Jesus for protection. We know that He is a present help in times of need.

Gentrification would be the word to describe our neighborhood. Since the presidential complex was built, at least five hundred people in our area have permanent jobs. Legalizing drugs did not diminish the number of drug addicts on the streets. Street drugs are still sold to local druggies because legal drugs cost more. While waiting for a bus near my house, a drug addict attempted to inject me with an HIV-laced needle because I only had change in my pocket to give him. I asked God to send the angel who protected me before to protect me again. For a second time, Jesus sent an angel to guard me. Whether it was the same angel, I do not know. The angel just moved me behind the perpetrator as he lunged at me. The addict dropped the needle and accidentally stepped on it. When he turned around and saw the angel and me standing behind him, he ran away, looking terrified.

I am sixty-four years old now, and I have lived a wonderful Christian life blessed with a beautiful Christian wife, two adorable children, and three grandchildren. My entire family and I actively participate in various church ministries and activities. Although I have watched the world become more wicked, I am thankful for the miracles Jesus has performed in my life.

The implanting of a chip in our hand or forehead is eminent. If you do not allow the implant, you will lose all rights to be a citizen in the world community. The implantation of the chip also means that you pledge allegiance to the Antichrist and denounce Jesus as Lord and Savior. Just like Joshua, as for me and my house, we will never take the implant of the Beast. There will be no independent nations; the Antichrist will rule a global community. If anyone does not comply with his edicts, their head will be cut off! A false prophet will demand that all people worship the Beast; there will be no other religions, only the world religion of the Antichrist.

Around midnight, my wife and I had just finished our nightly prayers. We prayed longer than usual because of the installation of the Antichrist the following week. While we were still on our knees, we heard loud shouts. Was someone being attacked on the street? Before getting up from our prayers, we heard a loud trumpet sound. The trumpet sound was blaring, loud enough to wake the dead. It sounded like a warm-up rehearsal before a music concert. Then, "IT" happened; my wife and I were caught up in the air at warp speed. We looked down at our bed, where our clothes were folded neatly. What were we wearing? We wore long robes with sashes. Our arms were stretched out in front of us as we flew higher and higher. My wife and I smiled at each other, enjoying our ascent to heaven. We saw angels, our children, grandchildren, neighbors, and church members looking around. We looked like characters in a Superman movie. I felt light as a feather; it was wonderful. We could barely make out a figure gleaming in white clothing standing on a cloud. As we flew closer, we recognized our Lord and Savior, Jesus.

BIG HOMMEY: HELL

I am James Williams, aka Big Hommey. My gang of misfits never knew my real name nor my real address. Accompanying them on their criminal missions was never my practice. Protecting myself was all-important. I hated them because I hated myself. How could I want them to be imprisoned or killed? It was easy because I had made my choice: I chose the dark side. Never knowing my parents kept me disconnected from society and vulnerable to predators. Deplorable, reprehensible, unpardonable, and shameful would be the words to describe the orphanage and my foster parents: monsters. They abused me in every conceivable way: sexually, physically, mentally, and emotionally. All I thought about was revenge. By the time I was twelve years old, I was totally depraved. No one wanted to adopt me because of my age and my track record of being rebellious and belligerent.

Finally, a real Christian family adopted me; but they had too many rules. I was expected to do chores, participate in Bible study, and attend church twice a week. I must admit, I was treated better than at any time in my life. I still defied them by refusing to do my chores and actually putting my fingers in my ears when they read the Bible. My punishment was to eat dinner in my room. Are you kidding? I would be strung up in some foster homes, literally, and beaten. I did not want anyone to be nice to me and certainly not try to convert me from a sinner to a Christian.

After I finished eating a scrumptious dinner in my room, Jesus Himself appeared to me. I was not afraid or reverent to Him; I remained defiant. Jesus talked to me and told me that if I accepted Him as my Lord and Savior, I would have had a wonderful, fulfilled life from now until I died at an old age. Jesus attempted to show me a video of my future if I accepted Him.

Although I was curious, I was too stubborn to look. I closed my eyes. Jesus quoted me a Bible scripture. Isaiah 55.6 -7, "Seek the Lord while he may be found; call on Him while He is near. Let the wicked forsake their ways and the unrighteous their thoughts. Let them turn to the Lord, and He will have mercy on them, and to our God, for He will freely pardon." I did not respond, I rejected Jesus, and he departed from me. Five minutes later, a dark figure appeared to me; he laughed and laughed. He told me that I should follow him and do his bidding. Together we could make all people pay for my ill-treatment by society. I embraced him and became the boogeyman.

My life of crime began when I killed my foster parents, Helen and Gary. I knew Helen had tranquilizers in her medicine cabinet because I would snoop around at night. I pretended to repent of my rebellious ways and asked for forgiveness. They were so happy. While they were preparing dinner, I crushed tranquilizers in their soup. They were knocked out in about an hour; I used the entire bottle. I cut their throats. I am sure they did not feel anything. Deciding the scene was not bloody enough, I disremembered their bodies with tools from the garage. My rage was finally quenched; I had inflicted vengeance on innocent people. I was sent to an institution for the criminally insane. After twenty years, I convinced a naïve psychiatrist that I was harmless. I was unleashed on society. I founded a gang of young misfits, and I exploited all of their insecurities. After using them for a few years, I would move to another state and start all over again with a fresh group of recruits. I had no sympathy for them or their victims.

I was only threatened when I saw the outline of an angel catching a bullet that Marcus shot at his menu item. I did not kill Marcus, which was my practice when someone failed to follow my orders; Jesus warned me not to touch Marcus because he belonged to Him. Marcus was the reason I got caught by the police. I was about to pass the helm to Leroy after he passed the test to prove he was ruthless enough to kill someone at random without considering collateral damage. Delance drove, and Leroy rode shotgun; I was the passenger in the backseat calling the shots. Marcus came out of nowhere, running and screaming for Leroy to stop. In the excitement, Leroy shot Marcus without realizing who he was. Marcus was four years older, taller, and heavier. The bullet changed directions and lodged in the right side of Marcus' chest instead of his heart.

Leroy realized it was Marcus and tried to help while crying uncontrollably. Unfortunately for us, new shot spotter technology, which could identify where the gunfire was occurring, led to a police officer in the area arriving at our location within minutes. The police caught us in the act. I never realized how close the friendship was between Marcus, Leroy, and Delance. Leroy and Delance never ratted on Marcus, but they sang like two blackbirds about me. They were given a deal; I was sentenced to life without parole. I must have gotten soft in my old age of forty years because I did not show the police evidence I had against any of them: my insurance photographs. As fate would have it, Delance's father heard I was in prison and paid an inmate to shank me because I had recruited Delance.

One minute I was being shanked; the next minute, I was in a damp, smelly dungeon. What the Hell? I heard a voice say, "exactly." This is not what I expected. Where were the strippers, death fighting, raucous card games, and orgies? These are the activities people did on earth when they were sinning. Where was my father the devil? The minute you thought something down here, the answer materialized immediately. Satan appeared to me. He looked hideous, not at all how he looked when he first appeared to me. He smelled like rotting flesh; his skin was scaly, and his nails were long. His body was misshaped, and his eyes were red slits. He laughed at me. He could not stop laughing then he disappeared.

I heard music: gangsta-rap and hard rock. The volume got increasingly louder until it was deafening. I put my hands over my ears, but it did not seem to help. Another sound caused my head to explode. Crickets or buzzing flies were incorporated into the music. The organs of my body responded to this last buzzing sound. My heart, lungs, and brain seemed to leave my body. It finally stopped. Thank God. Did I say that? I heard people calling on God, Jesus, and the Holy Spirit: too late. There seemed to be no atheist in Hell.

I was hot and thirsty. My feet were burning! The fire traveled upward until I was utterly burned up: only ashes were left. Why didn't I die from smoke inhalation? At least the excruciating pain was over. I was finally dead for good. This had to be a dream or a horror movie because the ashes rejuvenated, and I was whole again. That is when I noticed these creatures. They walked like gorillas, but they were really fast. They carried bats, big rocks, and a morning star. It was a spiked ball mounted on a shaft. These demons started beating me. I felt every blow. Screaming and begging for mercy caused them to beat me harder and faster. Why was I not dead? I forgot I was dead and in Hell.

My torture stopped for a while, and I looked around and saw and heard what was going on in the surrounding area. Hell seemed to be a vast amphitheater. There were sections illuminated periodically. One section seemed to consist of people groups. Sodom and Gomorrah were clearly marked. Another section held especially brutal world dictators. I could make out the faces of Adolf Hitler, Idi Amin, Stalin, Genghis Khan, Benito Mussolini. In the same section were serial killers: Ted Bundy, Jeffrey Dahmer, John Wayne Gacy, Jack the Ripper, Charles Manson, and many more. They were being drawn and quartered. Screams and screeching were all I could hear from them. There seemed to be no pause in their torment. Another section held people who worshipped false gods, liars, deceivers, and the sexually immoral. There was a Bible scripture describing them, Romans 1:29-32. I was a part of this group. "They have become filled with every kind of wickedness, evil, greed, and depravity. They are full of envy, murder, strife, deceit, and malice. They are gossips, slanderers, God-haters, insolent, arrogant, and boastful; they invent ways of doing evil and disobeyed their parents. They have no understanding, no fidelity, no love, and no mercy."

The last group I saw surprised me because they were people who attended church dutifully, were well-known church leaders, and were moral people; but did not accept Jesus as their Lord and Savior. They were not born again; they went through the motions. Some did not believe in anything or anyone. They were the when you are dead; you are done group. A Bible scripture appeared to answer my questions. Mathew 7:23. "Not everyone that saith unto me, Lord, Lord, shall enter into the Kingdom of heaven; but he that doeth the will of my Father which is in heaven. Many will say to me in that day, Lord, Lord, have we not prophesied in thy name? And in thy name have cast out devils? And then I will profess unto them, I never knew you, depart from me, ye that work iniquity." This last group seemed to have more of a reprieve from the torment.

My advice to you is not to come here. Hell is Hell. Do not rationalize your sin, including your unbelief. Seek Jesus while he may be found. Isaiah 55:7, "Let the wicked forsake his way, and the unrighteous man his thoughts: and let him return unto the Lord, and he will have mercy on him, and to our God, for he will abundantly pardon." I regret not accepting Jesus' invitation to a wonderful, saved life. I must get ready for my next round of torture. When I hear the music, I know another round of torment is beginning.

Chapter 4

NAMAZZI: PROTECTED

I am Namazzi. I am now eighteen years old. Many older people, young adults, and teenagers have moved to the big cities because they fear the Jaraiders. I still live in our small village and help my parents maintain our farm. I encouraged my family to stay in our village, not fear anyone, only to have unfailing faith in Jesus Christ, our Savior. Our protecting angel is still guarding our home and our whole village. I teach the preteen children basic math and reading.

Most importantly, I teach them the Gospel. There are fifteen boys and eight girls who help their parents with farming chores. These children are my family, whom I love and would protect with my very life.

Jaraider soldiers have not come to our village for many years; however, one night, the Lord gave me a vivid dream where an angel gave me precise instructions as to what I should do immediately. I dressed hurriedly, went to each home, and gathered all the children. Their parents assisted me in getting them dressed and ready for our trek through the dense jungle at three o'clock in the morning. Although the jungle was dangerous, especially at night, the angel told me that we would be protected and that I should follow a faint light that would illuminate our path. Thank God the children were between ten and twelve years of age and had the stamina to walk seven hours non-stop without complaining. We arrived at our location at about eleven o'clock that morning. The people at the missionary sanctuary greeted us warmly. We would be safe there; even the Jaraiders were forbidden to enter the premises. Missionaries live in safety until they are given their assignments in remote villages where they preach and provide any needed assistance. Some of them have medical backgrounds.

Later we found out that the Jaraiders had raided our village at dawn looking for children to kidnap "recruit" as child soldiers and slaves. The soldiers were outraged when they discovered the children were missing. They searched the jungle for hours, believing we could not have gotten that far away at night. The Lord Jesus caused them to walk around in circles until they ended up back at our village. They were livid, but they did not harm anyone. They just made threats against me and took food from the farmers. This was highly unusual if not unheard of because they would have maimed and even murdered people in any other village under the same circumstances. Remember, our guardian angel was there, and I am sure they sensed his presence. I have been divinely instructed to take my children to our country's largest, most populous city, where a dwelling would be provided for us. I obeyed God.

BONAMI: REDEEMED

My name is Bonami which means strong soldier; what a joke. The Jaraiders kidnapped me when I was eleven years old. If you are not familiar with them, I will tell you a few facts about them. They are a militia group who invade villages after an airstrike; they are paid terrorists as far as I am concerned. The name Jaraiders means devil on horseback, how apropos. After entering our village, they killed my father, uncle, and all of the men in our village. I felt as though my heart had stopped beating. As if that was not horrific enough, they raped several women and girls; finally, they kidnapped me and my friend Kwame to be child soldiers. My two-year nightmare began.

I used to be a happy child working with my father, farming, and caring for our animals. Three days a week, a teacher came to our village and taught us English writing, math, and history. I excelled in writing, and I loved learning new vocabulary words. A doctor also came to our village once a month. Our life was wonderful. Missionaries had come to our village and lived with us a few years ago. Everyone accepted Jesus as Lord and Savior. I could not imagine a life more wonderful; we loved everyone in our village and considered each other as family.

Now, I want to die. Every day I am beaten and nearly starved to death. Our leader Mombasi is especially brutal; he is the devil incarnate. In one village, he chopped off the arms of several children because they had been vaccinated against smallpox. He had a pet name for his machete, Moojida. Before committing a gross atrocity, he would say, "my trusty Moojida is going to be very busy today." He offered the children a choice, long-sleeve or short sleeve, which meant amputation at the elbow or the shoulder. How depraved is that? Believe it or not, there is a sociopath even more degenerate than Mombasi, the supreme leader Hugalo. I never understood their main objective except to kill and maim as many civilians in countries they deemed their enemies. I heard they had killed three hundred thousand innocent villagers in just a few years.

I could not murder. Attacking innocent people with machetes, beating them with tree branches, or stoning them to death was just too barbaric for me. I am a Christian. They gave me opiates and made me smoke marijuana. "Don't worry, little warrior; drugs will lessen your fear and cause you to be brave in battle." I never became brave in murder, but I was always high; everything was blurry and dream-like. I felt myself becoming desensitized after witnessing so many acts of savagery. That is what overexposure can do to a person, and our enemy, the devil, knows it.

We went on a recruitment crusade to a nearby village where we took food and kidnapped two twelve-year-old boys. Our leader did not recruit boys younger than twelve after Kwame committed suicide. Mombasi intended to kidnap a little girl old enough to cook, clean, and wash to be our slave. A young girl about eight or nine years old lived in the village. As we walked near her hut, we felt a foreboding; it was so intense that even Mombasi trembled and ordered us to leave the village immediately.

After all the opiates, marijuana, brutal beatings, and little food, I still could not use a machete on anyone. I beat people with my fist and tree branches, yet I could not cut someone with a machete. Why was I not able to take my life the way my friend Kwame had done. Mombasi said that I was a real disappointment to him and that I would have to prove my loyalty or be killed by him and all of my fellow soldiers. He said I must obey him without hesitation. He had to be sure I could be counted on to partake in a major initiative in the city, and then we headed toward **my** village! This is when I would make my stand, when and where I would probably die before my fourteenth birthday.

When we entered my small village, I saw my mother, sister, little brother, and all the wonderful, loving people in my home village. It had been over two years since I had seen them; they thought I was dead. Mombasi grinned that malevolent smirk. I observed the same smirk when he was about to perform an insidious atrocity. I knew that I would die protecting my family. Looking around at my fellow recruits reassured my suspicions that no one would help me. The villagers started praying and crying out to Jesus. They lay prostrate on the ground. I had never seen anything like this before. My mother told me to pray to Jesus to intercede for us. I did not ask Jesus to help me because I did not feel worthy of his intervention. I had dishonored Him too many times and committed too many sins. I had never used a machete, but I grabbed one from one of the other soldiers. Mombasi laughed and told me, "instead of coming toward me, you had better kill your mother. If you disobey me, I will cut off her head, cut your little brother in half, and dismember your sister limb by limb." I was not intimidated; I inched closer to him. An invisible force pushed me back far away from him. Mombasi dropped his machete and tripped over a stone. He was moving his lips, but no sound was coming from his mouth, and he was flailing around grabbing for his machete. He attempted to pick it up from the wrong end and cut himself: a real deep slash. It was like a scene from a horror movie. We all stared in awe as he bled profusely. No one said a word; there was stunned silence. We were all in awe, marveling at what God had done. Mombasi walked off into the jingle. He was mute, blind, and bleeding. My fellow soldiers were confused and disoriented. They did not know what to do. I told them to find their way back home, not just physically but emotionally and spiritually. That is what I intended to do.

My family and I packed our necessities and departed for the refugee camp that very day. It was a seven-day journey, but we knew where to stop along the way. We applied for emergency rescue relocation. After about one month, we were eligible to relocate to Melbourne, Australia. I related our story to the counselor leaving out details about my involvement when recruited by the Jaraiders. I am sure he had an idea about what I had done: I am equally sure he knew that I was not a willing participant.

My family and I were given a small furnished apartment near public transportation. The Christian church was within walking distance. My mother was offered a job in a daycare center, and my sister and brother attended school in the same building where my mother worked. I am an apprentice to a printer who provides copy for a local newspaper, and I also attend school, majoring in journalism. Before and after service, I clean the church; I want to show my gratitude to Jesus for forgiving me and saving my whole family from a horrific death.

It took quite some time for me to accept God's grace. I kept praying for forgiveness. I kept revisiting different scenarios when I could have just rejected Mombasi's commands. I should have allowed him to kill me. I did not have to take drugs, smoke marijuana, or brutalize people. Acknowledging that I did not stand up for Jesus was not easy. Finally, I prayed to the point that I knew Jesus bore all of my sins when he died on the "Cross," and He received the punishment that I deserved. I can lift my head and not be ashamed. Thankful is the word to describe me now. Redeemed is the word I would use to describe what God has done for me.

NAMAZZI: RAPTURE

I am Namazzi; My twenty-three children and I went back to our village and said goodbye to our parents and friends. I knew in my spirit that we would never see them again until we all went to heaven. Pick-up trucks were provided for us, and we arrived in the capital city. I know how Moses must have felt when God told him to leave his country, not knowing what would happen next. As soon as we exited the trucks, a very handsome man asked me if my name was Namazzi. I said yes, and he told me to follow him. The children looked at me as if I were crazy. I felt at peace when I looked at him. He was the pastor of a small church where he took us to freshen up and rest. After talking for a few minutes, I discovered that one of our villagers had told him what happened and asked him to assist us in any way he could.

He told me that the Lord told him to have us move into an old fortress near the church that had been vacant for years. It was dreary, dreary, dreary! It had an iron door, metal shutters on the windows, and a roof made of clay and concrete with steel rods. It looked impenetrable. I prayed and asked God what I should do: I was told to move in as soon as possible. We worked tirelessly for weeks, made a one time-payment agreement with the electric company, and graciously accepted donations from church members and nearby neighbors.

Living in that dreary fortress proved to be the best years of my life. That handsome pastor and I got married and raised our twenty-three children as if they were our own biological children. I worked in a nearby hospital, and my husband worked in a glass factory while the children attended school. We planted a garden in the backyard. Things could not have been any better. All of the children got saved and were filled with God's Holy Spirit.

One night we were all in the great room we used for our worship time together when we heard loud rapping on our door. We did not look out to see who was causing the commotion. My husband and I both knew someone wanted to harm us. The metal shutters were covering the windows, and the door was iron. We heard cursing and gunshots. Since we were already gathered together, we dropped to our knees and started praying. We asked God to deliver us from whoever wanted to harm us. The enemy was at the door using sledgehammers and pickaxes to gain entry. They attempted to start a fire to no avail. Finally, we heard heavy-armored vehicles pulling up close to our door. Someone said, "ram it until it comes down." I knew they did not just want to kill us; they could have bombed us if that were the case. They wanted to torture us and put our bodies on display. It had to be the Jaraiders seeking revenge for that fiasco in the jungle. It had been three years! I must admit this time, I was scared, my husband was scared, and the children were terrified.

We prayed and pleaded with God to save us. Above the noise, we heard a louder voice shouting something; we could not make it out at first. We heard noise reminiscent of an orchestra warming up with a thunderous horn section. Wait a minute. We heard our name being called; we just knew it was the Jaraiders with a sophisticated device that called your name and played music simultaneously.

Then it happened. All of us flew right through the roof, and we were flying above our building. I looked down to see soldiers, Jaraiders soldiers armed with assault weapons and machetes, enter our home. There were at least a hundred of them and a few city policemen standing across the street. All of the soldiers entered our house. I was flying so high at a top speed. I could not see clearly what was happening; however, I saw a massive explosion. The church, our home, and the structure on the church grounds were demolished. Fortunately, all of these structures were unoccupied. As we were ascending higher and higher, faster and faster, I noticed we had on robes with sashes around our waists. I saw a cloud that was lit up like a Christmas tree. Other people and angels flew closer to this beautiful cloud with lights swirling around it. We saw a figure standing on that cloud waiting for us. We all knew it was Jesus!

Chapter 5

PAULO: REDEEMED

My name is Paulo Souzza. You met me about sixteen years ago when I attempted to rob innocent little children. At that time, lightning came down from heaven from a cloudless sky, striking my gun and knocking it out of my hand. The little girl I attempted to rob looked past me and stared at something that caused her to open her mouth in awe. I did not see anything. It was such a weird experience that I decided to do something worthwhile with my life. I was unsure what I wanted to do, but being a gang banger was not it. I found a job at a shoe company that made high-end shoes for an American company. I had to lie about my age to get the job. I worked hard for a menial salary; however, the company provided lodging and food. I decided to distinguish myself from the rest of the workers by lining up the leather pieces precisely before double-stitching each seam. My supervisors acknowledged my exemplary work by promoting me to manager. At seventeen years old, I instructed older workers, always being patient and respectable. One day the owner of the company came to inspect the factory and noticed how courteously I taught the other workers.

Calling me aside, he asked me what my ultimate goal was for my future. Out of nowhere, I said I wanted to design a sewage system for the jhuggi. I will tell you if you do not know what a jhuggi is. I would describe jhuggis as vertical housing projects; at one time, ex-slaves squatted in them. After slavery was abolished, poor, unemployed people moved into these illegal residences. Can you imagine raw sewage from the apartment above you passing through an open channel in your kitchen? Naturally, drinking water and water for crops are contaminated while emitting an odorous stench. Disease spread rapidly. There is no running water or indoor toilet facilities, which exacerbates the problems. Cholera and dysentery are common illnesses in the jhuggis. There are at least one thousand jhuggis in my country. Murder and other crimes are seldom solved. Since people in the jhuggis pay no taxes to the government, the government feels no obligation to help them by providing necessary services, such as fire protection, police, utility installations, or repairs. The people who live in jhuggis cannot afford to improve their living conditions; the conditions are deplorable.

The owner of the high-end shoe company asked me if I had ever considered being an architect. I lied again and said yes, but I could not afford to attend university. I was given a five-year scholarship to complete my degree in architecture. I excelled in school, realizing my superior intelligence. After graduating, I agreed to work with the Help Humanity Initiative (HHI).

It was awesome. I worked with other architects, plumbers, and scientists to design a sewage system for the jhuggis. After three years, we began constructing an enclosed exterior sewage system, indoor toilets, and running water in each apartment in each jhuggi. Relocating people for several months while reconfiguring their homes was not easy, but we accomplished it. It took seven years, hundreds of millions of dollars, and tireless workers who often volunteered their time and expertise to rehab the jhuggis. I spearheaded the entire project keeping expenses under projected cost. I was so proud my name was a household word. Almost single-handily, I had vastly improved the lives of thousands of people.

All I heard was, "Paulo Souzza, we love you." I almost felt as if I could walk on water; I had not been to the beach lately to check whether I could. Maybe I could be cloned. Needless to say, I was a classic workaholic narcissist. I had no social life at all; however, I did meet a young lady who invited me to her Pentecostal church. Learning about different people in the Bible was so cool. I even imagined myself as some of them. I read my Bible daily and gave myself Bible facts quizzes. I did not feel I had to get saved because what could Jesus do for me? I was super intelligent, good-looking, and rich. My pride was about to cause me to lose my life. To use an antiquated term, I was about to get my comeuppance.

I thought about Nebuchadnezzar in the book of Daniel in the fourth chapter. Nebuchadnezzar said, "Is not this the great Babylon I have built as the royal residences by my mighty power and the glory of my majesty?" Even as the words were on his lips, a voice came from heaven. "This is what is decreed for you, King Nebuchadnezzar; your royal authority has been taken from you. You will live with the wild animals and eat grass like the ox. Seven times will pass by for you until you acknowledge that the Most High is sovereign over all kingdoms on earth and gives them to anyone he wishes?" The king was driven away from people and ate grass like the ox. His body was drenched with the dew of heaven until his hair grew like the feathers of an eagle and his nails like the claws of a bird.

I should have paid more attention to what happened to King Nebuchadnezzar, but I did not. One night I left the opera early because I did not want to get thronged by the crowd leaving the theater. I jumped into my Lamborghini, not noticing a gang of six teenagers hiding in a nearby alley. They surrounded my car so quickly I could hardly believe it. They demanded my wallet and my keys. Two of them had a gun pointed directly at my head. They were doing the same thing I had done to others when I was about their age. I laughed uncontrollably; I could not stop laughing. Apparently, I was the only one who thought the situation was funny. Just as I heard the click of the trigger, everything stopped. I mean freeze-frame on steroids. There was no movement, only stunned silence. I heard a voice; someone was talking to me. "Paulo Souzza, this is the Lord." You can bet he had my full attention.

"Do you think you accomplished anything on your own? I control everything. I have orchestrated your life. I did not allow the angel to strike you with his sword when you attempted to rob those little children; instead, lightning knocked the gun from your hand. Do you think you changed your own mind about leaving the gang? Who was responsible for your showing initiative at the shoe factory, causing the foreman to notice you? Why did the company owner give you a five-year scholarship to become an architect? That answer you grabbed out of nowhere to redesign the sewage system of the jhuggis came from me. Who do you think persuaded wealthy investors from all over the world to give money through the HHI to rehabilitate the jhuggis? I, the Lord, made you wealthy and successful. You did nothing on your own. I control the very breath in your body. I am the Way, the Truth, and the Life."

I was undone and did not deserve to live any longer. Shame, embarrassment, remorse, and humiliation only begins to express my emotion toward myself. I told the Lord how sorry I was for my unmitigated arrogance, and I begged God to forgive me. I pleaded for mercy and a second chance; I did not want to end up like King Nebuchadnezzar or, worse, dead. The Lord told me I was to become an evangelist/financier paying the expenses of ministers who wanted to fly to other parts of the country teaching the gospel and ministering to poor people. I was to give testimony to inspire others, especially young, disadvantaged teenagers. I gladly agreed.

When real-time returned, both guns misfired several times. People were beginning to exit the theater and started shouting at the young hoodlums. "Don't shoot him; that is Paulo Souzza." The whole gang ran away, fearing the crowd. The next day I joined a church and asked God to save my soul and fill me with His precious Holy Spirit, and He did.

Eventually, I asked the young lady I had been dating and with whom I had been attending church to marry me. I spend my days fulfilling my promise to my Lord and Savior, Jesus Christ. I am so humbled and grateful for a second chance. I still do not understand the gift of grace, but I am glad to be a recipient. How could God forgive me and bless me? I robbed everyone, even children. I even shot people. There is one thing I know for sure; salvation is not rational. It made no sense for God to forgive me after my despicable life of crime and extraordinary arrogance. I now realize that when Jesus died on the cross, He bore all of my sins past, present, and future, leaving me blameless and justified. It is never too late to sincerely repent and ask Jesus to forgive you and become the Lord of your life. I praise God because I am redeemed.

ARRYSHA: RAPTURE

Hello everyone. My name is Arrysha; I live in a beautiful South American country. It is not important how you begin your life, but how you live your life. I am a Christian who believes in the Father, the Son, and the Holy Spirit. My brother, sister, and I could have been shot years ago because we did not have money to give to teenage robbers, but God sent his angel to protect us. No one saw the angel except me. I do not know why; however, everyone saw lightning strike the gun the robber was holding.

Overall, life has improved drastically in our country because a brilliant young architect designed a sewage system concatenated with indoor toilets and running water. It has made all the difference in the world. There is no longer raw sewage causing deplorable unsanitary conditions resulting in the rampant spread of disease and death. The architect's name is Paulo Souzza. He looks so familiar to my siblings and me. We just cannot figure out where we met him. Paulo Souzza founded a free university for underprivileged youth. I took full advantage of his generosity by attending and graduating with a doctorate degree in nursing. I operate a nonprofit clinic caring for poor patients who live in the jhuggi. My husband is a doctor; we have three children and a one-year-old grandchild.

One day a man walked into our clinic complaining of reoccurring migraine headaches. The Holy Spirit granted me the gift of discernment. I knew something was wrong. I prayed to the Lord Jesus for protection and wisdom. After praying, I felt at peace. The Bible verse, "no weapons formed against you shall prosper," kept reverberating in my head. After questioning my new patient about the frequency and intensity of his headaches, he stood up suddenly and pulled a live grenade from his pocket. He said he was told to blow our clinic to smithereens. I had not heard that term in quite a while. I remained calm and began praying for him. He was taken aback; I asked him why he wanted to kill us, and he replied because his father Satan, told him to do it. The staff and patients had quietly left the clinic, but I continued praying for his soul. Eventually, he quietly left the clinic with the grenade still in his hand. Everyone returned, and we all praised Jesus and thanked Him for protecting us from the demon-possessed man.

We heard a loud noise a few minutes later, and the ground shook violently. Had he pulled the pin on the grenade near us? The earth stopped shaking, but we heard loud shouts. At first, they were incoherent. The sound became closer and closer to our location. I clearly heard my name, "Arrysha, come up here." People looked around to see from where the sound was coming. Other names were also being shouted. There was a loud trumpet blast, but not exactly a trumpet. The sound got louder and louder: closer and closer. Could this be the Rapture of the Church? I did not have to wonder for an extended period of time before I was flying in the air with my arms in front of me. I flew through the roof of my clinic. Some patients and staff were flying next to me. My husband, siblings, children, and grandchild were all smiling and flying. We were dressed differently, comfortable, loose-fitting garments. There was no opposing wind but a mild jet stream at our backs, projecting us upward. Finally, after what seemed like a long-time, we saw vibrant colors, pearlescent gates, shining streets, and someone standing in midair with their feet on a cloud. It was our Lord and Savior, Jesus Christ. All I could think of was the refrain of my favorite song: Jesus, Jesus, Oh how l love Him.

Chapter 6

LEILANA: PROTECTED

I was nearly stung by poisonous puffin fish when I was eight years old. God's angel picked me up and carried me to the beach. Now I am eighteen years old, and I am an apprentice learning how to predict sporadic disturbances on the ocean floor. I am studying at the University of Hawaii, majoring in marine seismology.

One day my diving group and I motored out several miles from the shore to study a phenomenon on the ocean floor. I was one of the divers who listened to sounds on the bottom of the ocean. On this particular day, we all signaled to each other when we heard unusual sounds. We decided to surface as soon as possible; however, we could not surface immediately without suffering the bends. The bends, also know as DCS or Caisson occurs when there is a rapid release of nitrogen gas from the bloodstream causing bubbles in the bloodstream. The bends can result in a coma or death. The noises got louder, and we did not know what to do. We signaled to our boat above us, but they did not know what to do. We prayed to Almighty God to help us.

We felt our bodies slowly moving in the water; the boat above us was also moving. How could this happen? We were being moved vertically and horizontally at the same time. After approximately half an hour, we were able to surface safely. What a surprise when we climbed into the boat; we were far across from where we had first stopped. Turbulence was coming from the bottom of the ocean; it felt like an earthquake. We docked quickly. We scrambled out of the boat and ran into the nearby mountains. There was an earthquake, and we would have been killed if we had still been where we first dropped our anchor.

Thanks to God Almighty, we had been moved supernaturally to safety. We had been spared from disaster and certain death.

LEILANI: RAPTURE

I am Leilani, who was rescued by God's Angel from the deadly sting of a pufferfish. God also rescued my diving team from an earthquake that began near the location where we were diving. Thanks to God. I graduated from the University and became a marine seismologist.

After graduating, I decided to work for the weather service; I work with geologists and geophysicists in a marine laboratory. The work is very challenging and requires dedication. It is such an important job and vital because we predict catastrophes, thus saving lives. Dr. Charles Richter, the most famous seismologist, invented the Richter Magnitude Scale, which determines the magnitude of an earthquake. Our team uses seismographs and computers to help generate graphical models of the earth's vibrations. All seismologists are especially concerned about the San Andreas Fault. The strain has been building for one hundred and thirty years and can produce an earthquake that could cause a tsunami at any time to crash into Los Angeles and San Diego. Tsunamis have struck Hawaii, Alaska, and the United States west coast on March 11, 2011, causing millions of dollars in damage and loss of life.

One morning while I was working in my lab, that still small voice, I believe is the Holy Spirit, told me to look at my computer. My computer registered a significant fall in the water level in the Pacific Ocean. My colleagues and I raced to the shore, where we saw the ocean receding rapidly. We knew that big waves or even a tsunami was about to happen! I prayed to the Lord Jesus to help me and give us time to warn people and save lives. We sounded our earthquake/tsunami warning and the verbal alert system warning. We told people where to go for shelter. They had to move uphill above the maximum reach of the tsunami. My team and I helped evacuate nursing homes, hospitals, and people who lived in low-lying areas. It had to be God's will because we were able to evacuate everyone in record time before the tsunami hit our island.

As a result of my noticing the recession of the ocean, which I believe God called to my attention, many lives were saved not only physically but also spiritually. Many people were so afraid they would die. They wanted to be saved before it was too late.

Several years later, my family and I were sleeping at the beach outside our house. The weather was delightful. I woke up, and I just lay there, thinking about the goodness of Jesus and how He had rescued me all my life. I felt so grateful. I heard a loud shout and the sound of a trumpet. Someone called my name, my husband's name, and my children's names. It sounded like someone on a loudspeaker at an event in a sports arena. "Leilani come up here, Aalika come up here, Aakamal come up here, and Kalani come up here. We were flying in the air, and we had on different clothing. I looked down and saw my house, my lounge chair, the beach, all empty. We were on our way to Jesus!

Chapter 7

MARIA: PROTECTED

I am Maria, who was kidnapped and rescued by God's angel who caused the motor to fall out of the captor's car and all four tires to go flat at the same time. I was the only one who saw the angel, but I was unafraid even before I saw him. After being drugged, I awakened in the back seat of my enslaver's car. My secuestrador's name was Fernando; I looked into his eyes and silently communicated what God had promised me. God told me that I would not be harmed or marred in any way and that I would be released. I knew that Fernando understood, so I started singing praise songs to Jesus.

I am twenty-six years old now, working for a social service nonprofit agency. My husband and I have two young children; my family encourages me to fight against the scourge of human trafficking. Dangerous does not even begin to describe what I am endeavoring to accomplish. The authorities are of little help; some of them are corrupt themselves, and others are just too afraid of the cartels. Selling girls and boys is so lucrative that the drug cartels often forgo selling as many drugs as they have in the past to invest in the prostitution of children and young adults

Initially, I approached my mission by educating young people in the church and school; warning them about trusting strangers, meeting people on social media, and applying for jobs in wealthy countries. I stressed that these jobs do not exist. Several young people listen, thus avoiding a wretched, wasteful, drug-addicted existence. After careful research, my team and I discovered the names of some despicable predators. They were usually cartel members; sometimes, they were coyotes who illegally transported people across the border. Some were government officials and law enforcement officers.

One day, I received an urgent call about three elementary school girls who had run away from home to get a lucrative job in America. Fortunately, it had just happened. My small but mighty group of five women and three men found the location where the children were being held before they would be sent to another location for grooming. I do not mean hair, nails, and make-up! They were being held in a run-down farmhouse far from town. We stood outside that farmhouse and called those criminals out. They ignored us at first, but we called them again. Come out and bring our children in the name of Jesus; we demand you to come out. Pedro Gonzales Rodriguez came out. I knew him, a recruiter of young children for use and abuse by cartels. I had seen him attempting to lure young girls and boys away from their families, promising them high-paying salaries in rich countries: telling them how they could help their low-income families by sending money back home. He loitered around schools, playgrounds, malls, and markets, always smiling and buying children ice cream and candy. Persuasion and feigned sincerity were his strong suit, a smooth operator. I often walked up to his naïve group of recruits and told them the truth. He hated me, and I knew it. I often wondered what kind of man could have no empathy for young children, some as young as eleven years old. Did he have parents, or was he an orphan? Did he have siblings, a spouse, or children? Was he a sociopath, or had he sold his soul to the devil? I did not know the answer to these questions, but I know that God can change a person's heart. Pedro had a smirk on his face when he exited the farmhouse. "What do you want, Insignificants?" We want you to return our three little girls. Four heavily armed men came outside pushing the little girls in front of them. Pedro said he would kill us and that no one would ever find our bodies and that the girls were his property.

We stared at him, and he stared right back at us. We had an authentic Mexican stand-off, but my fearless group of social workers/prayer warrior crusaders stood our ground. We told him again to let our children go. It reminded me of Moses demanding Pharaoh to let the children of Israel leave Egyptian captivity. When Pedro realized that we were not leaving without our little girls, he ordered his henchmen to shoot us. We did something unexpected; we dropped to our knees and started praying to Jesus to touch Pedro Gonzales Rodriguez's heart, to soften it, and let our children go. The men lowered their guns, but they started mocking us, saying, "oh Jesus, let our children go." I began to fear for my life and my warriors. What would happen to our children and our spouses? Would they ever find our bodies? Then I had an epiphany. Whenever I took my mind off Jesus, I feared for my life; but when I thought about how Jesus delivered me over ten years ago from kidnappers and how King Jesus died for me, I became emboldened and fearless. I kept my mind on Jesus and kept repeating the Bible scripture: No weapons formed against me shall prosper.

As the gunmen raised their weapons, a huge angel stood in front of us with his sword drawn and looking as if he was awaiting instruction from Jesus. The perpetrators turned pale, dropped their weapons and ran. Pedro started shaking, petrified, needless to say. We took our girls and left. The angel was still there looking at Pedro. I do not know what happened, but I do know that there is no way we will ever stop attempting to rescue young victims from human trafficking. We cannot allow children and young adults to be duped into a life of depravity, misery, and addiction. We will continue to work for Jesus and trust him for our protection.

PEDRO: REDEEMED

My name is Pedro Gonzalez Rodriguez, formerly a member of a dangerous drug cartel. Instead of search and rescue, my mission was to search and destroy. When social workers /evangelists stood their ground and started praying for God's intervention for the release of three young hostages, I laughed. Five women and three men, all unarmed, demanded I return their three children to them. I ordered my four associates to shoot them. Out of nowhere, a colossal angel appeared in front of them with his sword drawn as is if ready to strike! I wet my pants; I was scared half to death. I knew the cartel would probably track me down and murder me if I left their employment. That angel stared at me for a long time after everyone else had gone. He seemed to be waiting for instructions. After looking at me warningly, he lowered his sword and disappeared. Wow! I was scared straight. At five years old, I witnessed both of my parents being murdered by the cartel because they wanted our land to grow drugs. My ten-year-old sister managed to escape, but I was too slow and startled to run. I was in shock. The cartel enslaved me, making me work twelve hours a day on the farm. My clothes were inadequate, and I did not get enough food. No one cared. No one petted me, hugged me, or said one kind word to me for thirteen years. They treated the farm animals with more affection than me. I did not believe in God or His Son Jesus. When I became an adult, I was more animal than human. "Abtenor" is what I became a procurer of human bodies and souls. I persuaded young innocents to leave their homes and go to America and other rich countries, which offered free education and gainful employment so they could send money to their poor parents. I performed my job with flawless perfection. I am ashamed to tell you how many children and young adults fell victim to my silver-tongued persuasive lies. Human trafficking is quite lucrative, especially for the cartels. Did I have any sympathy for my victims? The answer is no, probably because I never received affection after my family was gone. How could I recruit children, some as young as eleven, knowing they would be beaten, tortured, starved, and constantly sexually abused? I did not know what to do with myself, having always worked for the cartels. Since I was gifted at persuading people, I became a used car salesman. Everything was okay for a while. I cheated people, and I lied about our cars. The car lot owner and I were in cahoots conspiring against our customers. There was a clerk who did all of our accounting. She and I became friends; she was a sincere born-again Christian. What an odd couple we were. She constantly warned us about our unscrupulous business practices. We should have listened because an irate customer demanded his money to be returned; he shot at me when I refused. I ran, and I never returned to the dealership. I found myself sitting in a church with my friend from the dealership. I listened to what was being preached. After everyone had left the church, I just sat there thinking about my life. I was a miserable excuse for a human being. I spoke aloud and told God that I hated myself and was ready to serve Him if He accepted me. Believe it or not, God spoke to me audibly. "Pedro, I want you to kidnap children for me." What? "You have expertise in how the cartels operate. I want you to sneak into facilities where hostages are held and lead them to safety." I looked around to see whether someone was in the church talking to me.

"Pedro, stop looking around to see who is speaking to you. It is I, Jesus Christ, who came in the flesh." They will shoot me before I get within five yards of their structures. "You will not be shot because I will make your enemies sleep soundly until you are completely gone. Read I Samael 26:12. King David takes a spear and water jug near King Saul's head. No one knew about it, nor did anyone awaken until long after David was gone. This is what I will do for you. "I will provide you with safe passage." I rescued four young teenagers from the cartel's holding facility that very night.

Four years have passed, and I am still rescuing young people from the cartels. I am known as "fantasima astuto" the sneaky ghost, and there is a fifty-thousand-dollar bounty on my head. They have no idea that I am Pedro Gonzalez Rodriguez. The Lord Jesus has led me through dangerous mountain trails and scorching deserts. A still, small voice would tell me which trail I should take and when I should seek shelter.

After rescuing five boys and two girls, a thirteen-year-old told me that I resembled her mother's uncle. Their last name was Rodriguez, and her mother had escaped the cartel after witnessing the murder of her parents. Her little brother could not run, so he was captured. I could not stop crying when I realized that I had rescued my niece. This precious little girl led me to my relatives. Reuniting with my sister, aunts, uncles, and cousins was the most wonderful day in my life. They hugged me and kissed me until I felt smothered; they made up for my lack of affection since I was five.

I will continue rescuing hostages designated to be trafficked by the cartels. I know that Jesus has forgiven me, and I know that he loves me and will continue to protect me. I am blessed. I am thankful. I am Redeemed.

FERNANDO: REDEEMED

My name is Fernando Ortega Lopez; where I live is dangerous. I should know because I used to be one of the people who made it dangerous. Kidnapping young girls and selling them to the cartels was my line of work. I was callous and unfeeling; I could care less what happened to them after receiving my money. The only time I had a problem was when one of those Christian girls kept singing worship songs to Jesus. She would not stop singing; she may have been a choir member. She knew the words to at least fifty songs: Bless the Lord Oh My Soul, How Great Thou Art, You Are A Shield For Me, etc. It was endless. This particular girl was not just defiant; she was assured, fearless, and confident. There was no fear in her eyes. She looked at my partner and me as if we were non-entities. She dismissed us because she knew we had no control over her. I heard a voice in my head say, "Do not harm her. She belongs to me, free her!" I did not know what to do. I usually scare my captives by knocking them down and cursing at them. I had a feeling that if I knocked her down, she would bounce back up like a Bobo doll I used to own when I was a child. How could I get rid of her without upsetting my partner? We would not get paid if we let her go. I did not have to wait long before my opportunity presented itself. When we stopped at a traffic light, the engine fell out of my car, and all four tires went flat at the same time. I told her to get out. My partner and I agreed to waive our finder's fee because she was too scary. She walked out slowly without looking back at us; she never stopped singing. We were relieved to be rid of her.

A few years passed, and I conducted business as usual until an eighteen-wheeler hit my car, causing me to have four broken bones and vision loss in my left eye. During my lengthy rehabilitation in the hospital, a minister started visiting me and telling me about Jesus. I told him that I knew about Jesus because my family and I attended church dutifully every Sunday and Wednesday evening for as many years as I could remember. My parents were pretend Christians: liars, cheaters, and drug dealers.

They opened a produce store where you could do one-stop shopping; you could buy your tomatoes and cabbage at the same place you bought your marijuana and cocaine. Are you ready for this? They justified their hypocrisy by tithing ten percent of their profit from selling illegal drugs and using an unbalanced scale to sell produce.

My parents were the biggest deceivers in the world. I did not know sincere Christians existed because some of the other parishioners were in partnership with my parents. I am sure that all of our church members were not hypocrites, but I did not try to find out who they were. Being a vulnerable child, I just assumed all Christians were insincere. Parents do such a disservice to their children when they are not honest. I grew up believing Christianity was an organization, a social club where families go and pretend they are something that they are not. The vocabulary is the same with each Christian: "God bless you, I love you brother, and I pray for you." What a joke. It would have been fine with me if my parents were honest sinners. I know that is an oxymoron. All the so-called Christians I knew were deceitful; they acted, looked, and spoke like everyone else. The exception was that sixteen-year-old girl and that minister at the rehab center. If I ever became a Christian, I wanted to be like them.

A few years passed, and my health drastically improved, but I did not learn anything from my ordeal. Although I was half-blind, I started kidnapping girls again. On my way home from a very profitable delivery, my night vision betrayed me, and I found myself in a river. I could not get out of my car! I just knew I was going to die this time. The next thing I did was pray; it shocked me to hear my voice praying to Jesus and asking for forgiveness. I promised God that I would live for Him if he saved my life.

The Lord Jesus sent three men to open the car door before it filled with water. I kept my promise to Jesus by becoming a real Christian, not a hypocrite. Working at a small mission helping recovering drug addicts to assimilate back into society is my life's work. I read the Bible to my attendees, telling them my testimony. I am thankful and I am redeemed.

MARIA: RAPTURED

I am Maria. The last time I talked to you, I told you about my life's endeavor and spiritual mission of stopping human trafficking in my country. God sent His angel to prevent us from being shot and to retrieve three young girls from the cartel. Thirty years have passed, and my small group of fearless warriors have experienced many successes; however, our job has become even more perilous as the world has become more and more depraved. People have been attacked on the streets in the daytime. Murders are hardly ever solved. There are no safe neighborhoods. My warriors and I do not fear; we pray because we know that God is still in charge.

A policeman arrested me today for talking to a group of young people to prevent them from following a trafficker. The policeman said I was inciting a riot. While in jail, I met a woman who was a trafficker; she was really nasty to me. She cursed me and called me a holy -roller, do-good – expletive, expletive, expletive. She told me that she was not going to be in jail long because she knew people in high positions of authority. I thought to myself, the policeman who arrested me is probably one of them. I felt the urging of the Holy Spirit to witness to her. I started telling her about the time I was kidnapped and the Mexican standoff. I prayed silently for Jesus to open her heart, and He did. She pretended not to listen at first, but after about three hours of non-stop talking, praying, and singing spiritual songs, she started crying, "God could never forgive me." She repeated this several times. I assured her that Jesus had already forgiven her and paid the cost of all her sins when he died on the Cross. She sincerely repented and asked for forgiveness from Jesus; she repeated the sinner's prayer.

We slept on our bunk beds for several hours. After what seemed like a long time, we both were awakened by someone shouting and calling our names. I thought it was someone in the jail calling us for the midnight court or something. We heard our names being called again; "Maria Gomez and Esperanza Morales, come up here." There was the sound of music, a trumpet or a French horn. In a nano-second, we were both flying in the air; we looked down at our jail cell. This was the "Rapture of the Church." Esperanza was being Raptured, although she had just gotten saved a few hours ago. I thought about the thief on the Cross next to Jesus, who recognized Him as the Lord of Lords and the King of Kings. The thief asked Jesus to remember him when he came into his Kingdom. Jesus told him that he would be with Him in paradise: Luke 23:43. I was so happy for Esperanza, but by no means am I a proponent of people waiting until the last minute to get saved. In Isaiah 55:6-7, the Lord tells us to seek Him while He may be found and to forsake our wicked ways and even our unrighteous thoughts and to turn to Him. If people continue to reject our Lord, I am afraid that He may allow their hearts to be hardened.

Remember, Pharaoh hardened his heart and would not let the Hebrews leave Egypt: Exodus 8:15-19. God hardened Pharaoh's heart in Exodus

7:3. I do not even pretend to understand everything in the Bible, but I know it is dangerous to harden your heart when God asks you to obey. The Apostle Paul warns us in Romans 1:25-28 that if we do not believe the truth, which is Jesus, after a period of constant rejection, Jesus may turn us over to a reprobate mind. A mind that causes you to have strong delusions so that you believe the lie. Finally, in Revelations 22:11, the Apostle John tells us that there is no second chance for repentance and salvation after you die. "He who is unjust, let him be unjust still: he who is filthy, let him be filthy still: he who is righteous, let him be righteous still: he who is holy, let him be holy still." When you feel that God is calling you, do not turn from Him. We never know when we will breathe our last breath or when the Rapture will occur; always be ready.

Esperanza and I kept flying higher and higher; we flew straight up toward a lighted area. There was no wind or atmosphere, no gravitational pull. I could breathe easily, and I felt as light as a feather. As I got closer to the lighted area, I could see a robed figure with outstretched arms. It was my precious Jesus.

Chapter 8

DR. PATELA: PROTECTED

I am Dr. Patela, a pediatric surgeon who used to be an unscrupulous, money-grubbing criminal who dismembered and blinded children for monetary gain. The Lord Jesus has been so gracious to forgive me and spare my life when I was such a despicable person. Since that angel stood before me with his sword drawn, I repented sincerely and refused to commit these atrocities ever again. Refusing to do the bidding of the criminals who hired me has proven to be quite a dangerous decision. Threatening to murder my family, exposing me to the authorities, and intimidating me by standing in my office at all times of the day has been hard for me to endure. There was a brief period where we practiced détente. I looked the other way when I saw children about to be abused.

Evil men did not entreat me to perform operations; however, I knew that the God of the universe wanted me to fight them. Waging war against them by naming names of other doctors and kidnappers would be a formidable task. I knew I was living on borrowed time; I caused many criminals to be convicted for their crimes against children.

One night when I was getting out of my car to go into my house, someone jumped out from behind the bushes and placed a towel over my nose and mouth; someone else grabbed me from behind. Soon I was completely unconscious. I was driven far from the city before the car stopped. Groggily I exited the auto. At least eight luxury automobiles were lined up in an open field. Some vehicles had two or three occupants. They all stood outside of their cars and glared angrily at me. They were going to murder me!

As I looked around my surroundings, I noticed a large pit in front of me. One of the culprits told me that I had one last chance to stop cooperating with the authorities and to work for them again. I said no emphatically. Someone threw a rock into the pit; I never heard it hit the bottom. Although I was scared and trembling, I prayed to God out loud. I knew prayer was the only thing that would save me now. I said, Lord, you said you would be my shield and my fortress and that I abide in the shadow of the Almighty. I recited the ninety-first Psalm verbatim. They all started laughing. I reminded the Lord that He had saved that little girl from me, and now I needed Jesus to save me from these evil vultures. I reminded God how I had changed my life to become a faithful Christian and a crusader for righteousness.

I did not have to wait long before a massive angel stood in front of me. I breathed a sigh of relief. What happened next was surreal. I watched these evil men, a cabal of wickedness, run past me with their arms outstretched to push me into the pit. They did not see the angel nor me. They all fell into the pit. They screamed loudly as they realized what was happening. I was reminded of the time in Luke 4:29 when Jesus walked through a multitude who attempted to throw him off a cliff. I looked around and saw no one. They were all gone, including the angel. Explaining what happened and describing how I felt is impossible. I had just experienced a miraculous deliverance, although it was terrifying seeing those who attempted to kill me run to their own deaths.

I know God sent His angel to protect me by making me invisible to them. I know that Almighty God wants me to continue fighting crimes committed against innocent children. I drove home in one of those luxury cars and parked about a block from my house. No one ever questioned me when the other automobiles were found near the pit. The bodies were never recovered from the pit because it was too deep. All of the people in my country who exploit children are not gone; they will never be gone until Jesus returns during his millennial reign. Several children will not fall victim to this wolf pack because they are gone forever. Praise God! Praise God!

DR. PATELA: RAPTURE

I am Dr. Patela from India, who refused to continue working for evil predators who maim children for money. That life is over for me. There is no amount of money in the world to ever tempt me to do that again since Jesus came into my life. After God's angel blinded the wealthy men who attempted to kill me and caused them to run into a pit intended for my demise, I continued working as a pediatrician and advocating for children; whenever I discovered people who wanted to exploit children, I exposed them. No one attempted to kill me again, although I received several threats. I never married; I devoted all of my time to saving children.

I no longer had much money because I practiced in a free clinic where poor children are treated. Ironically, some I had personally hurt. I am now sixty-five years old, and I have watched the world become colder and meaner. Very few people are even humane toward each other. There are famines more often than ever before; thieves steal food even from poor families. Christians are now called haters, and we are persecuted frequently. One of my patient's parents told me that four men were going to break into my house and steal what little I had and maybe even kill me. How can they target someone who helps everyone for free? It just spotlights the level of depravity to which the human race has sunken.

I had fought the good fight after my encounter with the angel and giving my heart and life to Jesus. I no longer live in fear. The Apostle Paul said, "to live is Christ, to die is gain." That is precisely how I felt. After bolting my door and windows, I decided to sleep on the roof. The stars seemed to shimmer brighter than ever; the sky was so beautiful on such a warm night. I do not know when I fell asleep. Suddenly I was startled and awakened by loud shouts; someone called my name. Was it the robbers? I heard my name being called again," Ravie Patela come up here." There was music from a horned instrument, a trumpet as if to announce a dignitary. Before my brain could comprehend what was happening, I was flying.

I was flying, going upward! As I looked around, I saw other people flying next to me. I recognized some of my relatives, church members, and young patients. The blind ones could see; those with amputated limbs were whole again. We were all smiling, and some of us were laughing and shaking our heads in unbelief. We were traveling so fast and constantly climbing higher and higher. Although it was pitch black outside, we were encompassed in a broad stream of light that got brighter as we flew upward. Then it happened. I saw Jesus standing on a cloud with outstretched arms!

Chapter 9

AMICA: PROTECTED

I am Amica, who escaped from a war-torn, ravished area of our country during a bloody civil war just before our house was bombed. God sent His angel to lead us to safety. We migrated to a nearby country where life is more peaceful and safer. Although the present government allowed us to migrate, they constantly harassed us and agitated us. Sometimes they conduct raids in the middle of the night demanding to see our papers; they also monitor our movements. Most of the citizens in our new country are hostile toward us. Many of them despise us because we work for lower wages causing them to lose their jobs or be demoted. They blame us for overcrowded schools, hospitals, and public transportation conditions. They are correct. My father did get another teaching position, and I work in a grocery store part-time after attending classes at the University. We are thankful to have enough money to live humbly. Bringing home dented canned goods, day-old bread, and other outdated food helps sustain us.

As my dad and I were about to enter our house, we noticed a strong, pungent odor. My mom and little sister ran out of the house; they were regurgitating and wiping their eyes. I felt nauseated, and my skin and eyes were burning and itching. All of our neighbors were in the street experiencing some horrible sicknesses. The government had leased townhouses to us in this rundown low-income area; it is all we could afford. We were immigrants who had to leave all of our possessions; we were blessed to have escaped with our lives.

Everyone began to panic, grabbing each other, screaming, and wondering what in the world had happened. Although my eyes were burning and my eyesight was blurry, I saw a man standing at the end of the block wearing a full hazmat suit. He carried a container similar to the ones used by exterminators. What had he done to us?

All of the Christians started crying out to Jesus. We reminded God that he had saved us before, and we knew he did not save us to allow us to die in the streets from poisonous gas; we pleaded with the Lord to send help immediately. He did just that! Momentarily a torrential rain drenched us. I have never experienced rain of this intensity. We could not see our hands before our faces for a few minutes. Our eyes and skin stopped burning and itching. We all began praising Jesus for sending the rain.

I noticed the man in the hazmat suit walking into a house. There was an explosion; I could see the smoke and flames through a large kitchen window. Honestly, I did not know whether he was injured or not. It is not clear whether he initiated the chemical attack on us, but I believe he was responsible. I saw him stagger out of the house, coughing and gasping for breath. I know for sure that God did not allow this weapon formed against us to prosper. The Lord Jesus heard our prayers and sent torrential rain from heaven to save us.

ABEER: REDEEMED

You do not really know me; my name is Abeer, and I was responsible for single-handedly attempting to kill all the immigrants in a one-block radius. Father God, Lord Jesus, and the Holy Spirit had other ideas. If you will remember, Amica and her family were rescued by an angel minutes before their house was bombed. Well, not only did her family migrate across the border to my country, but thousands of immigrants also invaded my country. Their presence exacted a toll on our educational, medical, and employment systems.

I was studying to become a full-time medical doctor. Having just become a physician assistant, I only had two years before becoming a full-fledged doctor with a medical degree in tow. You cannot imagine how disappointed and angry I was when I was told that an immigrant doctor would take my position, including my salary and university stipend. My senior director explained that our medical facility would benefit from the expertise of a medical doctor who had practiced for several years. This doctor had agreed to be paid at a salary far less than his actual worth. My demotion was only temporary until all the immigrants could be absorbed into our economy; I would be able to resume classes and regain my position and my stipend in about a year. I was livid! I had to move to a cheaper residence to make ends meet.

Deciding that day not to roll over and play dead, I devised a plan to systematically rid our town of these imposing foreigners one block at a time. Being a member of the medical community enabled me to access certain chemicals. I had studied contagious diseases and poisons. I knew that certain non-lethal chemicals could be mixed to form a deadly toxin.

My concoction was going to burn those intruders from their outside to their inside.

I obtained a hazmat suit and meticulously mixed my deadly brew, being careful not to come into contact with the mixture. While our new inhabitants were at work or at school, I pretended to be an exterminator spraying the deadly mixture around the base of each house. As soon as the newcomers entered their houses, they began to feel nauseous and hot. Their skin and eyes started to burn. I began watching and waiting for them to feel horrific pain in their lungs. Hopefully, they would all die a painful death, but that did not happen. All the residents were screaming in agony in the streets; then, the rain started. Everyone was drenched; eyes and skin stopped burning. They all cried tears of joy and thanked Jesus. That is all I could hear: "thank you, Jesus!!" I did not know this Jesus, but I knew a supernatural intervention had occurred.

After entering my house, I was distraught, and I accidentally put my exterminator apparatus near the stove; a fire ensued. It soon got out of control; my house was on fire! The rain helped to quench the flames, but my lungs were on fire from inhaling the toxic chemicals while attempting to save my house. I made it out of the house and managed to drive myself to the hospital where I worked. Apparently, my lungs were severely damaged. I was placed on a ventilator. One of the doctors whom I knew told me that I only had a short time to live. To my surprise, that immigrant doctor who had taken my position started praying for me. What? He prayed to this Jesus the Christians loved so much. Apparently, Jesus listened because I began to breathe on my own. After a few weeks, I was ready to leave the hospital; however, I needed around-the-clock care. My insurance was no longer viable because my demotion canceled the entire medical package. This immigrant doctor took me to his modest home, where he and his family took care of me as if I were a beloved member of their family. They ministered to me and read the Bible to me. If I sincerely repented, they told me Jesus would forgive all of my sins no matter how depraved they were. I confessed to Jesus, but not to the doctor and his family. I could not tell them what I had done, how I had attempted to kill all of them. I believe Jesus saved me from an eternity in Hell.

Eventually, I received my medical degree, and now I help everyone with no prejudice or enmity. Jesus loves all of us, and we should love each other. Jesus gave me a second chance. I am so grateful to be redeemed.

AMICA: RAPTURE

This is the last time you will hear from me. Although it was difficult, I completed my degree in elementary education. My passion was teaching young children because they are naturally curious and innocent. Children do not know how to be prejudiced unless they are taught to dislike and mistreat a group of people because they are different from themselves. I also taught Sunday school every week at our small Christian church. Since there were few eligible men in my community, I never met anyone I wished to marry. After eight years of bloodshed, most of the young men had been killed or imprisoned by the government. The majority of young women could not afford to attend University to better themselves to insure a more lucrative job. They struggled to make ends meet by cleaning in private homes and places of business. Single mothers would leave their children with grandparents while the mothers worked upward of twelve hours a day. A few marriages were arranged with relatives from neighboring countries. Young women jumped at the chance to marry and move elsewhere.

Unfortunately, we did not have any male relatives in our family with whom to arrange a marriage for me. Dedicating my life to Jesus Christ, my Savior, and teaching young children was the best decision for me.

Our world became darker and darker. There were continuous riots in the streets where stabbings and shootings occurred unceasingly; almost all the immigrants stayed close to home in their humble abodes.

I read about this man who was to be named leader of the United Nations. No one would tell us who he was, only that he would bring about world peace. Everyone was in awe of him. After reading in the Bible many times about the Antichrist, the son of perdition, I dreaded his inauguration, which was to happen within a few weeks. I thought to myself about how naïve people could be led astray so easily. There were wars between nations, ethnic groups, and family members. Female agricultural workers could not produce enough food for everyone in our nation. As a result of slower food productivity, people were hungry and angry. Gangs of young boys constantly robbed adults; they ruled several communities. Adults had to ask these youths for permission to conduct certain activities. The weather was unpredictable: frequent floods followed by sustained periods of drought and more storms. I knew we lived on borrowed time; these were the last days. When were we going to be 'Raptured?" I thought the sooner, the better. Violence was rampant; people were encouraged to always walk in groups. One night a group of young hoodlums knocked on doors trying to gain entry to homes. Their knocks sounded desperate, but no one opened their doors. A regiment of soldiers confronted the youth gang. The exchange of gunfire seemed endless. When the noise finally stopped, we looked out of our windows; dead bodies littered the streets. At least fifty teenagers lay dead. Soldiers took the hoodlums and emptied their pockets after kicking their bodies to make sure they were not alive. The soldiers just laughed and laughed. I knew living conditions were only going to deteriorate. Someone told my father that all churches would be demolished because the new United Nations leader decided that he and his prophet would establish a new world religion where people would only worship the leader, the Antichrist. I prayed for the Lord to get us out of this world. A few weeks after the massacre in the street, my family and I felt that we should pray unceasingly. We got on our knees, and we prayed and prayed for the souls of unsaved people everywhere, especially my beautiful six-year-old pupils and their families. They were my priority. We soon lost track of time. When we heard someone shouting, we all stopped praying and listened carefully. Were the soldiers returning to kill everyone in our immigrant community? No, it was not the soldiers; our names were being called. "Amica, come up here." I was confused. I heard it again, "Amica, come up here." I listened to the names of each of my family members being summoned. There was a piercing trumpet blast and a whooshing sound. Before I could wrap my mind around what was happening, I was flying in the air at warp speed, arms extending in front of me. I glanced around and saw my family, some of my neighbors, and my precious little pupils all flying right next to me. We whizzed above treetops.

A lighted pathway reminded me of the wake of a ship only going upward. I had never experienced such peace, tranquility, and total exhilaration simultaneously. Although I never had biological children, I felt the way an expectant mother must have felt at the sight of her newborn baby. Something even more spectacular was about to happen. I was not disappointed. Standing on a cloud with outstretched arms was our Lord and Savior: Jesus Himself!

Chapter 10

ELISAPU: PROTECTED

Ten years ago, an angel prevented my family and me from being attacked by a ravenous bear. I am now eighteen years old, and I am attending the University of Alaska to become a medical doctor. I am a volunteer, part-time search and rescue team member; we help people who send distress calls while mountain climbing.

Our team has rescued thirty people so far. Most climbers are well prepared to climb a mountain; however, few are prepared to climb glaciers. Climbers have boots with crampons, climbing helmets, climbing ropes, and ice axes. Few climbers have avalanche trans crampons. Often the weather changes quickly, significantly above the accumulation zone. There are crevasses where you can become disoriented above the accumulation zone; thus, losing the path and your footing.

One day we received a distress call from a group of glacier climbers because a group member had been covered with ice and snow during a small avalanche. When we arrived, they were digging frantically to rescue their friend. We helped them and rescued the climber who was alive but had a broken arm and leg. After securing him on a stretcher, we began the long, arduous trek down the glacier. The patient was blessed to have found an air pocket while buried under the snow. Our rescue team always carried medications, splints, and a portable stretcher; therefore, we were confident that our rescue mission would be successful. We failed to realize that it would get dark so early, nor anticipate a snowstorm. We lost the path, and at one time, we were dangerously close to the edge of the glacier. Everyone was afraid; however, I knew that God could save us. I prayed to the Lord Jesus to send His angel to assist us the way He had sent an angel when a bear was about to attack us.

God answered my prayer; we felt an invisible force gently pushing us closer to the middle of the glacier path. We began to see track marks that were not covered by snow. After what seemed like a few minutes, we were safely on the ground. Everyone was amazed we had reached ground level so quickly in the dark during a snowstorm. God had sent His angel to guide us safely down the glacier, protecting us from calamity.

I completed my education, becoming a medical doctor specializing in sports medicine. I still assist in search and rescue missions. One day a prominent sports superstar came to the hospital. His regular doctor was on vacation, so I had to care for him. After an x-ray, we realized his injury was more severe than we thought initially. A biopsy confirmed that he had cancer in his knee joint. He wept bitterly because he knew his career was over and depending on the severity of cancer, he might require amputation to save his life.

Unfortunately, his leg did have to be amputated; I felt so sorry for him. A week later, another patient of mine contracted a deadly virus and had to be connected to a ventilator where his odds for survival were minimal. Still, another of my patients lost her hearing because of a head injury despite wearing a helmet. I was so depressed; I started crying and telling God how helpless I felt.

A voice inside my head spoke to me and told me not to worry about my patients and stop being depressed. The Lord Jesus assured me that all people who die in faith would be Raptured, and people who are alive when He comes for us will be Raptured also. Everyone who is disfigured or maimed will be made whole. He told me to preach the "Good News" of the gospel to them. Immediately, I felt at peace. I know that Jesus will right every wrong and restore everything. I eagerly await the Rapture of the church.

ELISAPU: RAPTURE

I am Elisapu, saved from a bear attack and rescued from falling off a glacier during a rescue mission. I know that God protects his children regardless of their age.

At fifty-eight years old, I can honestly say that my life has been one of fulfillment and dedication to my Lord and Savior, Jesus Christ. I have administered life-saving medicine and care to numerous hikers and athletes. People do not realize that rescue workers and physicians risk their lives to save them. Intentionally veering off designated paths and climbing solo, prohibited everywhere and causes undo dangers to rescuers.

In the past few years, there has been an influx of wealthy people flying to Alaska and staying in five-star hotel resorts to climb glaciers. If the airports are inaccessible because of dangerous weather conditions, they pay exorbitant fees to daredevil helicopter pilots to reach these posh locations. Often, these wealthy people are arrogant, self-centered and feel that they should not be restricted by the same rules and regulations as everyone else.

One family paid a guide extra money to climb a glacier for longer than what was originally contracted. You can probably guess what happened. They got lost and had to call for a rescue with medical assistance because a teenager had fallen through a deep crevice. There was no team of fellow hikers to help this time, only another worker and myself. We were forced to make the dangerous climb to rescue these people.

When we finally reached them, we knew it was an impossible situation. The teen had fallen down so far we could not reach him without climbing down into the crevice because our rope was not long enough. The teenager's father was cursing God, spewing all kinds of profanity, and berating the tour guide. I had to still myself and pray. As I began to pray aloud to Jesus and beseech him to help us, the enraged father calmed down and started praying to God to save his son. He made a promise to God to serve Him the rest of his life if He would have mercy on their family. His wife, a Christian, was also praying. God told me to climb down on the rope and pull the boy up. I asked God whether He was sure, knowing that I would die if I were to reach for him. The boy's position was far from my natural reach. It took a literal leap of faith. While my colleague held a bright spotlight, I climbed down as far as the rope would allow. The boy was crying because he knew it was impossible for me to reach him.

God sent an angel who pulled the boy to my hands. The child's eyes appeared as big as saucers when we saw the enormous angel. After being pulled to safety, the boy told his parents what had happened; they were so grateful. My colleague is a Christian. The tour guide, the boy's father, and the teenager himself accepted Jesus as their Lord and Savior. We all rejoiced and thanked Jesus.

When I returned home, my family was asleep. I was so tired I went directly to bed and was sound asleep before very long. I was awakened by loud shouting. My husband was also awakened; our names were being called. "Elisapu, Eric, come up here," I answered, who is it? I heard another loud shout and our names being called again; this time, the shouts were accompanied by a blaring horn blast. Had someone hit my car and caused the alarm to be triggered? That did not make sense because who was calling our names? No one knocked on our door or rang our doorbell. "Elisapu and Eric, come up here." Faster than I could blink my eyes, I was flying through the air. I flew through the ceiling and the roof and past the accumulation zone. My husband, children, and grandchildren were flying next to me with outstretched arms; we all wore comfortable robes with sashes. I saw several patients and their families, including the family that was just rescued; coworkers and strangers were also flying. Angels seemed to be escorting us upward within a large stream of light. The brightest lights were ahead of us. We were moving faster than a jet plane. Finally, we began to slow down as we reached our destination. A luminous figure came into view, standing on a cloud right in front of us with the most beautiful smile I have ever seen. My heart skipped a beat. I felt pure love and overwhelming peace emanating from Jesus.

Chapter 11

KARL: PROTECTED

I am Karl, and the last time you heard from me, I was in a hospital recovering from a botched, black market kidney extraction. I am twenty-six years old; I was sixteen when I was butchered. You have heard the expression, "bought sense is the best teacher." Well, I learned from my self-indulgent, wicked misadventures. After recovering from massive blood loss, infection, and kidney removal in an alley, I sought Jesus.

Attending church service with my family was enlightening; it took only a few weeks for me to ask Jesus to be my personal Savior. After being saved a few years, Jesus called me to be an evangelist to young people seeking all kinds of physical gratification: drugs, deviant sexual experiences, and even occult practices. I stand outside nightclubs and bars preaching the Gospel of Jesus Christ. Some young people listen and change their lifestyle. Unfortunately, other young people ignore Bible teaching and dismiss my pleadings. They choose to engage with people who influence them to participate in unbelievable deplorable behaviors.

The proprietors of these establishments are not happy with me. I can imagine how the Apostle Paul felt in Ephesus when the silversmith led by a man named Demetrius started a riot because Paul's preaching against worshipping idols caused the lucrative idol-making business to diminish significantly.

Early one morning, I was returning home after preaching the Gospel all night outside a popular nightclub when a speeding car targeted me. All I could do was pray. I truly felt like a deer caught in the headlights; I could not move. Suddenly an angel stood in front of me! Wow! The car hit some invisible shield, wall, or something causing it to wreck as if it had hit a brick wall. The occupants of the speeding car were killed on impact. Jesus sent His angels to protect me by placing a hedge of protection around me, thus saving my life.

Even if God had not saved me from being run over by the speeding car, I am sure Jesus knew that I had already made up my mind to follow

Him no matter what might happen to me. I will continue to follow Jesus and teach His Gospel in season and out of season. I know God is able to protect me because He has done it several times. Whether I live a long time or only a short time longer, I will follow Jesus and continue to do the work He has entrusted me to do. Praise God –Praise God.

KARL: RAPTURE

I am Karl, who preaches the Gospel outside of nightclubs and bars. At fifty-eight years old, I am still being protected by God. I have brought hundreds of souls to Jesus because of God's grace and my relentless stand for Christ. The owners of these nightclubs still want to kill me, but after what happened to a group of bar owners when they attempted to murder me, there have not been any more attempts on my life.

As I was going home to my family one night, I felt I was being followed. First, one car would follow me; then, it would trade-off with another car. What was going on? Although I was not exactly afraid, I knew in my spirit that something was wrong. When I reached an intersection with a four-way stop, I took off after stopping. Two cars sped through their stop sign and hit my car simultaneously, one on each side. It was near midnight, and no one was around to help me. I was stunned and pinned in on the driver's side, but not injured. I heard a loud shout. I did not believe the men who hit me were shouting; they were both standing outside of their cars with assault rifles in their hands. I could not exit my car; it was so mangled. I was a sitting duck. Loud horns were blaring. The sound was not coming from my car. The sounds was eerie and piercing. The two assailants came near my car with one hand covering their ear and using their other hand to hold their riffle.

Someone called my name. Did they know my name? "Karl, come up here. Karl come here." Faster than I could blink my eyes my head started spinning. I was looking down at the crash scene. My clothes were folded neatly on the front seat, my glasses on top of my shirt. Was I naked? Was I dead? No! I was flying through the air! Looking down from the sky, I saw two men standing on either side of my car. If they had only looked up, they would have seen me in a long robe with my hands extending in front of me flying in the air along with other people. Angels seemed to be escorting us to heaven. All of us had our arms extended out in front us. This must be the way humans fly, not like birds with their wings extended at their sides. We seemed to be flying in a stream of light, like the wake of a ship. I was really enjoying my experience and reflecting on my life. What if that angel had not led my family to that alley when I lay bleeding? I probably would have died and gone to hell. I kept ascending higher and higher, then my heart skipped a beat and leaped for joy. I saw Jesus welcoming me home.

Printed in the United States
by Baker & Taylor Publisher Services